Burn

FOR ME

A FIGHTING FIRE NOVELLA

LAUREN BLAKELY

Entangled Publishing, LLC
2614 South Timberline Road
Suite 109
Fort Collins, CO 80525
Visit our website at www.entangledpublishing.com.

Brazen is an imprint of Entangled Publishing, LLC. For more information on our titles, visit www.brazenbooks.com.

Edited by Alycia Tornetta and Stacy Abrams
Cover design by Heather Howland

Manufactured in the United States of America

First Edition June 2014

For anyone who's ever loved a fireman...in or out of uniform...

Chapter One

As Jamie watched Smith work the party, shaking hands and smiling for the camera, she was sure it was some kind of crime to be that good-looking.

He had a sinful combination of smolder and charm, with his close-cropped dark blond hair, strong jawline, and pure blue eyes. And his body. Just kill her with its perfection. A body like that should be outlawed.

There was a reason he was the star of the fireman's calendar, and that was the same reason every woman here — and probably around the country, come to think of it — had a copy of the Hidden Oaks Volunteer Firefighters' Calendar.

Because Smith Grayson was gorgeous, and a glass of wine or two had a way of making her check him out more than usual.

"Hey, Jamie, you might want to stop staring, or Smith will think you actually like him."

Her cheeks flushed as she returned her attention to

her friend Kaitlyn, who leaned against the bar. They both worked at The Panting Dog—Jamie was the manager, Kaitlyn a waitress—but they had the night off and were here at the kickoff party for the town's upcoming Spring Festival that would lure a whole slew of tourists to Hidden Oaks. Jamie had organized the party, so she wanted to see how it turned out, and she was pleased with her work. Laughter and music rang through the bar, and spilled out into the wide and grassy town square, where the festival would be held in a week.

"I'm not staring at him."

"Right. And I'm the Queen of England, and these are my people," Kaitlyn said, gesturing widely to the crowd that filled the microbrewery. A new establishment, The Panting Dog had quickly become a popular watering hole in their Northern California town, known for its vineyards, boutique hotels, cute shops, and its absolutely fine men who put out fires.

"I always had a hunch you were royalty," Jamie said, grateful to segue into any other topic than the volunteer fireman she should absolutely, positively not be lusting after. The trouble was, Smith was always around. He'd been spending even more time than usual at The Panting Dog since the construction company he ran was building out the back of the bar. To top it off, she and Smith bowled together once a week at the local lanes with a group of friends. Bless those friends; they made it so she didn't really have to be alone with him. She could only imagine how that would work out—them bowling together, him trying to show her how to improve her form, standing behind her, slinking his arms around her waist, making her shiver.

Damn, why did her mind stray there when it came to Smith? She wasn't the type of woman who was given over to thoughts of lust, who let her body's physical cravings lead her on. Besides, she'd spent enough time around that man and had resisted him because he simply wasn't her type. She wasn't his type either. She was organized, a planner, devoted to her to-do list, and he was fly-by-the-seat-of-his-pants. She was the woman who didn't swear; he was the fireman with a sailor mouth. She wanted someone serious, someone studious, someone she could see having a future with. Too bad she hadn't met anyone in a long time who fit that bill.

A long, dry, aching drought of a time.

"You should just go for it with Smith," Kaitlyn said, nudging her with an elbow.

Jamie shook her head. "I can't and I won't, thank you very much."

"Oh, c'mon. You two can't stay away from each other. You're always chatting."

"No, we're not," she said, narrowing her eyebrows as if her friend were crazy. Though, admittedly, there was some truth to Kaitlyn's comment.

"And you're always hanging out together here at the bar, or at the bowling alley."

Jamie flubbed her lips. "We do not."

"And he's always giving you the eye like he wants you."

Her heart beat faster, betraying her brain. "Really?"

Kaitlyn's eyes widened, and she pointed at Jamie. "See? You're into him, aren't you?"

Jamie shook her head quickly, trying to deny the way her heart skittered with the possibility that he was attracted to her too. "I was just surprised, that's all."

"That's why your cheeks are all red and flushed."

Her hand flew to her face, and she could feel the warmth there.

Kaitlyn lowered her voice. "You're always looking at him like you want him too. So why not see if there's something to the two of you?"

Jamie sighed. "I can't. You know that. Look what happened to Diane when she got involved with a guy she was good friends with. I'd be walking down the same path of trouble she faces with her ex," she said, mentioning her sister's ex-husband. They were friends first, and even though he had a whole lot of notches on his bedpost, Diane took a chance on him anyway. A fireman a few towns over, he'd wound up trampling all over Diane's heart and marriage, and was one more reason why Jamie needed to stay far away from those love 'em and leave 'em types. A smooth one with the ladies, Smith had that same easy way about him, especially on nights like this, as he held court, telling a story to the curvy brunette, Lisa, who seemed to cling to his every word. A photographer for the calendar, she'd been snapping party pictures, and was now trying to glue herself to Smith's side. When she ran a hand down his arm, jealousy flared inside Jamie.

What the hell? Why on earth would she feel a sliver of anything? She had no reason to feel jealous, and she wanted to drop-kick her stupid envy right out into the night.

"He's not so bad. You should think about it," Kaitlyn said, her matchmaker smile lighting up her entire face. She couldn't resist trying to bring two people together, with a little nudge here, a nudge there.

"Nice try, but I am Not. Thinking. About. Him. One. Bit,"

Jamie declared.

She turned away from the scene and reached for her glass of wine as the music switched to Maroon 5. Good old Adam Levine would distract her from Smith. She'd listen to the song and get lost in the words. She finished off the rest of the chardonnay in a hearty gulp that she was sure would wash away all thoughts of the man she could never be with.

"Not thinking about whom?"

Oh crap.

The sexy southern drawl made her neck feel hot. That was the problem. Ever since she'd first met him, she hadn't been able to blot out the heat she felt when he was near. His voice alone made her skin tingle. Why did men who were totally unsuitable make a woman's body feel so good with just a few words?

Kaitlyn mouthed *see you later*, and slinked off.

Jamie swiveled around to face him. "Not thinking about Adam Levine one bit."

Smith wiped a hand across his brow in an exaggerated gesture. "Well, thank the lord. I was terrified your mind was wandering to the Sexiest Man Alive," he said, relaxing against the bar, looking far too good in his jeans and dark gray T-shirt that fit him so well. He ran a hand through his hair, and she found herself wishing that were her hand.

"My mind is wandering nowhere at all, except to another one of these," she said, tapping the edge of her wineglass. "But good to know you read *People* magazine."

"Of course. Gotta stay current on all the important matters at hand. Who wore what when and who's doing who," he said with a twinkle in his eyes and a flirty tone in his voice. She laughed at his comment; he'd always made her laugh. Life of the party, the guy who was fun, never too serious. He held up his index finger, signaling the bartender for another glass. "And I'll take one more of the pale ale."

"Coming right up," the bartender said.

"Now that we've established you're not thinking of rock stars, and that your mind isn't anywhere but exactly where you want it to be, are you having a good time tonight?"

"I am having an excellent time. I'm very excited for the Spring Festival," she said, doing her best to keep their chitchat friendly, because that's all they were—friends. They'd be no good for each other as more. Opposites in every way. She was a romantic, he was a playboy, she was wine, he was beer, she was poetry, he was…wait, did he even read?

Exactly.

So not her type. She read all the time. Everything from poems to romance novels.

"And what is it that gets you most excited about the Spring Festival? Is it, say, the scent of cotton candy in the air?" he asked in a mock serious tone, as if cotton candy were a very important topic.

"Of course, seeing as I'm the keeper of that sweet treat," she said, since she'd be running the cotton candy stand this year with her sister.

"I do love the *taste* of sweet things," he mused, then inched closer to her, meeting her gaze, speaking in a low and sexy tone, making it clear he was enjoying the word play.

"You do?" she asked, as a spark zoomed through her.

"Some more than others," he said, keeping his gaze locked on her as the bartender set down their drinks. He didn't stop looking at her as he tossed some bills on the counter.

"Like what?" she asked, unable to resist the suggestive back-and-forth.

"The ones that are sinfully delicious," he said, in a voice laden with innuendo. "The kind of sweetness you almost need to repent for."

Sinfully delicious. Those words thrummed through her, and she found herself hoping she was one of those sweet things.

Snap out of it.

When he raised his beer in a toast, she tried to steer away from the double entendres. She picked up her glass, clinked it against his, and took a drink. Her throat was dry, and she desperately needed the liquid. "To the festival," she said.

"To the festival."

"Tell me what else *excites* you," he said, and it was clear he wasn't talking about the festival.

But she needed to. She had to. Or she'd be fanning herself soon.

"Oh, you know. All the games."

"All those crazy games booths where you can win the stuffed animals?"

"Oh definitely. I've been practicing my bottle ring toss all year," she joked, miming throwing a ring, glad to find her way back to banter, because that's what she and Smith were good at. Innuendo? She didn't think she could manage that tonight, not with the wine already flowing in her veins, making the night feel smooth and buzzy.

"How about dunking a certain fireman in the dunk tank?" he asked, referring to his booth at the festival.

"I'll make sure you go down with a splash."

"All you have to do is hit hard," he said, downshifting to that slow and seductive tone, one that seemed to linger on that last word. "And I'll go down."

Oh holy hell, why did she have two glasses of wine tonight? It weakened all her defenses. Now she was right back on the first bus to Lustville, fueled by flirting.

That's how it went for the next half hour as she finished her wine, he knocked back his beer, and they chatted more about the party, and the music playing, and the festival. Even though Smith could never ever be her kind of guy, they'd always been able to talk about anything from the foibles of celebrities to the best technique for nailing a strike, from what makes a perfect microbrew to favorite desserts. Through it all, there was the common thread of ribbing and teasing, like the time a few months ago when he'd seen her on the side of the road changing a flat tire. He'd pulled over and offered to help, but she'd laughed him off as she twisted the lug nuts off. "I know what I'm doing, thank you very much," she'd said, as he leaned against the frame of his truck.

"I'll just stand and watch, then," he'd fired back.

"You do that and see if you can learn something," she'd replied with a roll of her eyes. Then the teasing stopped and he strode over to her.

"Let me do it, Jamie," he said, in a commanding voice, one that made it clear he wasn't going to permit her to do it herself. "I'm not the kind of man who's going to stand by and watch a woman change a damn tire."

Then he took the jack from her and swapped the spare tire on her car in minutes flat.

"All done," he said, and stowed the damaged tire and the tools back in her car, taking care of every single detail.

She knew how to change a tire, but she wasn't going to complain about not getting her hands dirty.

The music shifted over to a slow song.

"You should dance with me," Smith said. No flirting. Just a straightforward statement. It threw her off, the directness. Because it was the same way he'd talked when he told her he was going to fix the tire: in no uncertain terms.

"What? This is a party at a bar. It's not a dance."

"So? One dance," he said, resting his hand on the bar so near to her hand that she wished he'd inch closer.

She looked around. The Panting Dog was still packed, tables were full, and the bartender was busily serving up more drinks. The party likely wouldn't lose steam for another few hours, but she needed to cut out early, since tomorrow night she'd be back behind the bar for her regular shift.

"I really should go," she said, pointing to the hallway. "My purse is back there."

"Then one dance on your way out the door," he said.

She shook her head. "I don't want to dance in front of everyone. It would look weird," she said, her mind racing back to Diane and her ex-husband. He was always kissing her, touching her in public, wrapping her up in his arms and making it seem like she was the center of his world. What a lie that had been, since he was never truly serious about their marriage.

Smith leaned in, brushed his finger lightly against her wrist, sending a flurry of shivers down her spine. "Then don't dance with me in front of everyone."

"What do you mean?"

The noise and the crowd turned blurry, and Jamie's focus narrowed solely to him.

He tipped his head toward the unfinished section. "Dance with me alone. Back of the bar."

It wasn't a question. It was almost a command, and it was one she found she liked.

"Why?" she asked, her breath catching.

"Why do I want to dance with you?"

"Yes. Why?"

He stepped closer, his words only for her. "Because it's spring. Because the weather's beautiful. Because it's a lovely night. Because you are the prettiest woman here. No, wait. In the whole damn town. Because dancing is fun, and on nights like this, one dance can sometimes be the best part of the night."

Her stomach flipped like a pipsqueak gymnast. They were only words, but there was something borderline lyrical about them. Whether he meant them or not, she didn't know. But she liked the way they made her feel—sexy, pretty, carefree, and full of possibility, like this night.

Then his hand was on the small of her back—a light touch, but a thoroughly possessive one, as if he were marking her, and it was enough to turn her senses upside down. She shouldn't flirt with him, and she definitely shouldn't dance with him, because dancing could lead to her hands on his body.

Images flashed before her eyes. Her hands on his waist, the hard planes of his abs, his hips. Her holding on to him.

She didn't want to give in, but maybe if they danced just once—one dance, that was all—she would get him out of her system. She could say good-bye to this wild kernel of lust that ping-ponged through her body whenever she saw him. Prove to herself that the ridiculous attraction she felt for Smith was misplaced.

"Okay. Let's dance."

Chapter Two

He hadn't scripted out the night.

He hadn't come to the party to try to get close to Jamie.

But only because they were friends, and had been since he moved to town from Georgia a few years ago after he'd finished college. He'd restrained himself, knowing he wasn't her type, and wanting to keep her as a friend. Sure, they had fun together, and they could chitchat for hours like they had at the bar tonight. But he knew anything more was unlikely. She'd always gone for the more serious, more studious, more buttoned-up kind of guy.

But with the sheen of a buzz backing him up, a dance sounded like the perfect nightcap. He'd take what he could get, and just the chance to be closer to the woman he wanted would have to be enough.

When they reached the quiet back room, he pulled her in close, his hands on her waist, hers on his shoulders. Her fingers were restless, as if she was unsure where to place them.

"You ever dance before, Jamie Lansing?" he asked, unable to resist teasing.

"Yes I have, thank you very much."

"What kind? Ballroom? Swing? Salsa?"

She rolled her eyes, but went with it, grabbing his hand and positioning their arms together in a sharp line as if they were poised to tango. "Tango, of course," she said, and he threw his head back and laughed at her attempt. "Or would you rather we square dance?" she asked in a fake southern accent. "That more your speed?"

"Oh, make fun of my heritage, why don't you?"

She shrugged. "Can't resist," she said, mimicking his drawl.

"You are too much. Why the hell do I put up with you?"

"I could say the same to you," she tossed back.

"*Same*," he said and wiggled his eyebrows.

"You are such a goof. You're never serious," she said.

He rearranged his features in a dour look. "Better?"

"Maybe," she said, but she was smiling, so he tugged her in closer. "So how's the construction going? Are you almost done?"

He shrugged. "Soon, I hope. I've been getting calls to do other jobs, and would love to take them on too. But I'd have to hire some men before I do that."

"So hire some men to help you," she said as if the answer were that simple. And sure, it was that simple to her, and he got that. They were close friends, but he rarely shared the inside details of his business with anyone, even her. He kept certain things to himself. A man's work was a man's work.

"That comes with its own damn set of problems," he said, a note of annoyance creeping into his voice, though he wasn't annoyed with her for asking. He'd been wanting to expand his business and take on some new jobs, but the last time he'd hired new employees, one of them had stolen some jewelry on a job. Since then, he'd handled every job solo. Better to do it himself. The last thing he wanted to talk about was work, and problems, and the things beyond his control. He wanted to stay 100 percent focused on this moment and nothing more—the present was what mattered. "Besides, I'm all about avoiding problems. I don't care for them," he said, shooting her a lopsided grin. "Let's talk about something not involving work."

"Fair enough," she said. "No more work talk."

They danced silently for a moment, and she pressed her hands lightly against his shoulders, as if she were nervous to hold him.

"It's okay," he said, eager to take the teasing to another level. Jamie was always so buttoned-up and proper in how she spoke, never uttering a swear word, and he would love to see her loosen up. *With him.* "Your hands aren't weighing my shoulders down."

"I was terrified they were," she joked.

"Or were you trying to cop a feel?"

"You wish," she said with a pouty curve to her lips.

"Maybe I do," he countered, stripping away the sarcasm as they moved slowly in the dark corner to the sexy beat of the music, their shadows casting doubles of them across the exposed wood of the wall. His fingers wrapped around her hips, his thumb gently stroking her hipbone once, twice. Damn, she felt good.

She stiffened for a moment. "You do?"

"Maybe," he said with a shrug.

Why was it so hard to just tell her what he wanted?

Because he knew that if anything were to happen physically, she'd push him away. Especially once she heard the things that would come out of his mouth. He knew this woman and what made her tick — how fiercely she loved their small town and all the people in it, to how close she was with her sister, and most of all how she had a thing for poetry. He might not be a fan himself, but sometimes he'd peek at whatever book of poems she had her nose in at the time. He'd seen her reading once in the town square, and could tell by her contented sigh and the dazed look in her eyes that she liked the words.

"'And the blood of her veins in the moonlight throbbed to her love's refrain,'" he'd read out loud, over her shoulder. "Got a naughty little book there, Jamie?"

She'd promptly snapped the book shut and given him a sharp glare. "Wouldn't you like to know what I think is naughty."

Oh, yes he would. He would absolutely like to know what she thought in that department, because he wanted to know what she thought about nearly everything. He'd never gotten along so easily with a woman who was so very different from him. Besides, Jamie came from the perfect family, white picket fence and all, while he'd grown up an only child with two parents who cheated on each other and then divorced in a flurry of anger. He'd tried like hell to get them to stay together to no avail. He half wondered if that was part of what drew him to Jamie — she had all the things he'd longed for. She had a fierce devotion to her parents and her sister. But though he might admire her connection to her family, to this town, to her job, and even to her books, did that mean they were right for each other? He was a shoot-from-the-hip kind of guy, rough-hewn from the tougher circumstances of his childhood.

They might get along just fine, but deep down they were so different. That didn't stop him from wanting her, though, and he hadn't been able to get her out from under his skin since he'd met her. He found himself tugging her closer. He gently fingered a strand of her hair, touching the soft waves.

"Smith," she said in a low voice, half a warning, half an invitation.

"Yes?"

"You're touching my hair," she whispered.

"I know. And I want to touch more of you," he said, and his heart beat harder.

"You do?"

"I would love to have my hands all over you."

Her eyes widened and she pressed her hands against his chest, giving herself room to look him square in the eyes. "Is there something going on with Lisa?"

He was taken aback. "The photographer? Hell no. Why?"

"Because she was all over you out there," she said, tipping her forehead toward the party.

"No. No. No. No."

"Four denials?"

"I swear," he said, breaking the contact to hold up his hands, as if they were proof.

Yeah, Lisa had always been flirty with him. She was slated to shoot the annual fireman's calendar next month, so she was always hanging around, suggesting ideas for locations and even poses. *How about if you had one hand on the ladder and Becker was unrolling the hose?* Smith had simply shook his head. The calendar didn't need to be classy, but it needed less Chippendale and more of the rough-and-ready smolder that had made it a bestseller. Hell, the latter was why the battalion had been voted the hottest in the country, and Smith was damn proud of that accomplishment because all of the calendar proceeds went to the burn center at the local hospital.

"Why are you asking about her?"

"Just wanted to know…" she said, letting her voice trail off, and the lingering silence felt like some kind of invitation. She looked up at him and her pretty brown eyes held his gaze for a beat. Then one more. She swallowed and her lips parted slightly. She didn't take her eyes off him.

Holy shit. Did she want him as much as he wanted her? The possibility that this wasn't one-sided felt like a bolt of adrenaline shooting through his veins. He'd always figured she'd never give him the time of day. That he wasn't her type whatsofuckingever. But maybe, just maybe, there was a little something there for her, too. He had to seize the moment. Had to tell her. She probably could figure it out anyway, since she'd been snug against him a minute ago. He swallowed any fear, looked her straight in the eyes, and told her the flat-out truth: "There's nothing going on with her because the only one I want to have anything going on with is *you*."

She blinked several times, as if she didn't believe him. Or maybe she was just processing what he'd said. She raised an eyebrow, challenging him. "Really?"

"Yes. Why do you think I wanted to dance with you?"

"Because you're a dancing fool," she said, returning to their jokes.

But he was undeterred now. "I meant what I said about

you being the prettiest woman here and the only one I want to dance with," he said, then launched into the important question of the night. "If I kissed you right now, would you smack me or kiss me back?"

She shot him a sly smirk. "Why don't you find out?"

"I believe I will."

He threaded his hands through her hair, resisting the desire to pull hard and crush her mouth to his, knowing he'd need to take it slow with a woman like Jamie. He might want to devour her, to kiss her hard and fiercely, but he had to rein it in. Restraint was the name of the game. He'd never be the right guy for her the way he wanted to take her. Bite her. Do bad things to her. So he'd allow himself just a kiss.

He ran the tip of his tongue across her lips. He nipped lightly, tugging her lip in a way that made her gasp.

Slow it down, he told himself.

He brushed his lips against hers, holding back as best he could. She tasted so damn good though, the faintest bit of wine still on her lips. Her lips parted, inviting him in for more, and he swirled his tongue against hers.

The next thing he knew, she was backing them up against the wall. He responded by crushing his mouth to hers and twining his hands tighter into her hair. He kissed her hard, ruthlessly, wanting to consume her with deep, greedy kisses, but cursing himself for it. Jamie needed sweetness, tender kisses and touches. He forced himself to ease back, breaking the kiss. She whimpered at the lack of contact, but then he moved to her neck, layering soft kisses on her collarbone that made her sigh hungrily.

"Oh, Smith, that feels so good," she whispered.

She felt pretty fucking good to him too, so he nibbled on

her shoulder, and then she grabbed hard on his ass, bringing him close, and that did him in. He pressed his teeth into the sweet flesh of her shoulder, biting down.

He braced himself, figuring she would pull away.

Instead, she moaned softly, almost as if surprised. He pressed his lips to the bite mark, soothing away any pain.

"Sorry," he muttered.

"Don't be," she whispered. "Do it again."

• • •

She'd never been into biting. But then, she'd never been bitten.

Something about the pleasure and sweet, sharp pain drove her wild, though, and heat pooled between her legs, especially when he bit her again. There was the slightest bit of stubble on his jaw, and the bristly feeling of it against her skin ignited all her desire to be *taken*.

That word echoed in her lust-swamped brain.

She leaned back and stretched her neck to the side, inviting more.

Smith blazed a trail of hot kisses and sharp nibbles along her shoulders and her neck. She grabbed for his waist, pulling his body closer, so she could feel the weight of him against her, his trim stomach, his legs, and the best part of all—that fantastic hardness. She rubbed her thigh against his erection and ran her hands across the firm planes of his belly through his T-shirt. He hissed in a breath at her touch.

"Damn, woman, when you touch me like that, it makes me want to take you."

Her eyes widened. "Really?"

He pulled back to look at her, his voice now a low rasp.

"Yes."

"How do you want to take me?" Jamie had never been talked to like this before, but it turned her on, she was learning. She'd always liked the flirty way he'd talked with her, but that was just the tip of the iceberg with him. His mouth was so much dirtier than she'd imagined, and his words made her feel alive, electric. Somewhere, in the back of her mind, she knew better. But accessing that part of her brain was becoming difficult. Rational thought crumbled when he kissed her. Reasons to walk away fell through her fingers after he'd touched her.

"Hard. And fast. And up against the wall."

She'd never done it up against the wall. Sex was meant for bedrooms, by candlelight, with soft, sexy music playing. But her body seemed to think otherwise because desire unspooled in her—and so did her own patent curiosity to be with him. She'd figured one dance would get him out of her system, but that was child's play. To eradicate this man from her head, maybe she needed to do the deed once and for all. A one-night-only performance, and then she'd never have to think about him again. Yes, she reasoned—as much as she was capable of reasoning given the swirls of lust clouding her mind—one time with Smith and then she could wipe her hands of this desire that had lodged a permanent home inside her. She hoped this wouldn't complicate their friendship, but a one-night stand was safe, she reasoned. They could give in to the lust this time, and still be friends tomorrow, right?

Of course.

Besides, she liked the idea of being taken. Liked it a heck of a lot, judging from the way the hairs on her arms stood on end and her skin sizzled. "Storage room. Now," she said, in between pants.

She led him to the small room a few feet away. Once inside, she kicked the door closed, dimmed the light, and went for another kiss before she could think twice. Thinking was out of the question now. She'd made her decision—she was going for it. Taking a one-way ride on the Smith train and then she'd get off it for good.

She zoomed in on his abs again, running her hands across his stomach. My god, he was pure male perfection. He felt even better than he looked in the calendar—and he looked damn spectacular in those pages. She needed nothing more on this earth right now than to map his strong body with her hands. She yanked off his shirt so she could have free rein.

"Jamie," he warned as his shirt fell to the ground.

"What?"

"Are you sure?"

"Am I sure of what?"

"If you take off anything else, I am going to be fucking you. Got that? This is your warning."

She blushed at his crudeness. But it turned her on even more. She had no idea why, especially since she didn't use those words herself, so she didn't know what to make of her reaction, but she was aching for him. She trailed her eager hands across his pecs, so solid, so strong. "What if I don't want to listen to that warning?"

"Then I am going to need to find out if you're as wet as I think you are right now."

Jamie was used to Smith the sweet talker. Smith the flirt. Smith the upstanding fireman who saved people when they needed to be saved. But Smith the dirty talker? Who knew that would ignite her? She'd always wanted romance, sweet nothings, poetry—pretty words to make her swoon.

This was beyond swooning.

She was a live wire, and her veins were flooded with heat.

"I want you to find out how turned on I am," she whispered, fingering the hem of her skirt, half-shocked that she was inviting him in like this.

He arched an eyebrow, and perhaps he was surprised, too, that she was going along with everything.

"You better be," he said roughly, grabbing her wrists, and pinning them over her head, as he backed her up against the shelves. The wood edge pressed into her spine, and it should have hurt, but instead it was yet another sensation that reminded her of how hot he was for her, and vice versa. "Because if I take off your panties and you're not fucking soaked through, I am going to have to hold you down hard."

Her eyes widened in surprise with his words. She raised an eyebrow, feeling daring and risqué in a way she never had before. "Is that a threat or a promise?"

He grabbed a hand, lowered it, and pressed it against him. She moaned at the feel of his steely length through his jeans. "You think I'm joking?"

She shook her head, grinning like a lust-struck fool. "I want to touch you."

Who was this woman saying these things? But they were coming out of her mouth, matching his dirty words as best she could, as he rubbed her palm over his erection.

He shook his head as if he were tsking her. "You will, but first things first. Before I let you touch my cock, I need to know how much you want me. I need to feel how"—he leaned in, his mouth buzzing its way to her ear—"slick you are between your legs. I want your panties to be so damn soaked you can't put them back on afterward."

She was on fire, lit up all through her blood and bones and breath. Every cell in her body was comprised solely of desire and reckless need.

"*Please* touch me," she whispered, and he dropped her other wrist.

With strong hands, he gripped her hips and lifted her onto the shelf, shoving paper towels and washcloths to the floor in one quick sweep of a hand. He was commanding. He was determined. He was a man who knew what he wanted — and he wanted her. She might regret this in the morning. Hell, she might regret it in an hour, but right now there were no regrets.

She wanted him. She wanted him hard and wild. Like she'd never had it before. One time, one night.

"I'm going to make you come in my hands, and then I am going to take you."

Chapter Three

Jamie's panties alone—red lace with a white flower in the middle—were a turn-on. But the feel of them. They were so hot and wet that Smith had no choice but to rip them off. She spread her legs wide, and he felt her against his fingers and cursed. "Fuck, you're hot, woman."

"You made me this way," she said, her head falling back as she gave in, rolling her hips against his hand.

He wanted to thank his lucky stars that she was so willing to dirty talk back in her own way. He'd never expected her to, but she sure as hell seemed to be loving it, judging from how she felt against his fingers.

Drawing a slow, lingering line against her delicious wetness first, he then teased at her clit. She arched her hips against his hand, and her breathing grew erratic. Her blouse had fallen open along her shoulder and he planted another bruising kiss there, more teeth nipping into her skin. She bowed her back in response, and his mouth cruised over her throat to her full breasts, all while using his fingers to explore the hot flesh that called out for him. He stroked her swollen clit until she moaned so loudly that he reflexively glanced at the door. But he didn't really care whether anyone heard because she'd opened her legs wider, asking for more. He worked his fingers faster, then slid a finger inside her.

"Oh God," she gasped and her voice rose an octave.

Another finger, and her breath caught.

"You like that, don't you?"

"I do," she panted.

He pressed the pad of his thumb harder against her, rubbing circles that drove her into a whole new level of frenzy.

"I want to know what you look like when you lose control, Jamie. I want you to give it all to me. Fuck my hand," he said, and she responded, panting and moaning as she rocked her hips. "You smell so unbelievably sexy when you're this turned on," he said, starting to lose his mind with desire for her.

"It's all because of you," she said as she dropped her hand from his hips to his cock and stroked him through his jeans, driving him wild.

"You like that? You like how hard you make me?" he said, practically groaning into her ear because he was so damn ready for her. "If you touch me, you're going to need to finish me off, you know that, right?"

"I'm dying to feel you," she said, gasping out the words in an unsteady voice.

A low rumble worked its way up his chest as he crooked his fingers into her, loving how she gripped him with her creamy flesh. "You can only touch me after you come."

Her mouth fell open, and she bucked against his hand as he took her to the edge.

She screamed out a yes, grappling at his hips, his waist, to hold on tight as her orgasm crashed through her beautiful body. He rained kisses on her neck as she came down from her climax, savoring the taste of her sweet skin and the way she'd let go completely with him.

A minute later, she unzipped his jeans and reached inside, taking him in her hands.

He closed his eyes, hitched in a breath at the feel of her soft hand stroking his shaft. He'd pictured this many times, imagined Jamie touching him. But more than that, he'd pictured making her come on his cock.

He curled his palm around her hand, then took her hand off of him.

"I want you against the wall. And I want to know what you sound like when I make you come twice in one night," he said, scooping her up from the shelf and setting her on the floor.

She obliged, that wild look in her eyes telling him all he needed to know. She pressed her hands against the wall, and he was rewarded with the gorgeous sight of her skirt hiked up to her waist and her ass wiggling.

"Jamie." She looked at him over her shoulder and he smacked her ass lightly. Her eyes widened. "I want to look at you while I fuck you senseless," he said, turning her around. He took out a condom, rolled it on, and lifted her up against the wall, pressing her spine into the wood.

"You ready for me?"

"So ready," she said.

Then he sunk into her.

. . .

Jamie's head was fuzzy, and her body felt like it was vibrating. Somewhere, in the recesses of her mind, she knew this was a recipe for disaster. But she'd never had sex like this before. Hard, rough, all heat and need. She never knew she'd like it so much. That she'd love it so much. She wasn't a Goody Two-shoes, but her repertoire had been missionary and girl-on-top mostly, and never had she gotten it on in a storage room. Yet here she was with her legs spread in her place of work. The knowledge that she was mere feet away from the party she'd planned sent a charge through her, the riskiness leading her on.

She gripped his shoulders tight, holding on as he stroked inside her. He moved hard, just like he kissed. Possessively, hungrily, like he wanted to own her body. She could barely even move, but she didn't need to because he held her ass in his strong hands, all while filling her. Then he slowed his rhythm, making sure she felt every single exhilarating thrust, as his fingers dug into her flesh.

"I want you to feel all of me," he said, groaning into her ear. "I want you to feel everything as I fuck you deep, Jamie."

The world was fading out with his words. Wild tension gripped every corner of her body, like she was held taut with lust. She closed her eyes, let her head fall back with each agonizing stroke, climbing closer to another release. "I do, I do feel everything," she whispered in broken breaths.

"Look at me," he said harshly. "I want to watch you come. I want you to look at me when I come inside you."

She opened her eyes, his face a few inches above hers.

His dark blue eyes holding her gaze. She couldn't move, he was in 100 percent control of her—her pleasure *and* her body—and he was taking them to another level, insisting on closeness. It was so intimate now as they locked their gazes, the connection so intense they didn't need to talk anymore. No more directions, no more dirty words. She watched as his eyebrows raised, the strain and the tension written on his face, as he thrust in her, slow, hard, deep. She was coiled and tight inside, from the torturous pace, from the exquisite agony of another build, her body reaching for more, craving another climax.

"I have wanted you for so long, Jamie," he said, thrusting into her, his admission making her grab harder on his shoulders and pull him closer. "I'm so into you. Have been for so long."

"I've wanted you too," she whispered against his neck, all her truths so easy to say with her body awash in magnificent sensations.

"So." Another thrust. "Fucking." A hard drive that sent her spinning. "Long."

And then, like a switch flipped in her cells, she started to tremble as she felt all the tension release and there was nothing else in the world right now but this wild abandonment as her orgasm took over. She could no longer focus, no longer keep her eyes open. She held his shoulders, digging her nails in, and felt him pump his hips into her. Then his stilted breaths, his moans, his mouth on her neck, his strong hands on her ass, as he came inside her.

Soon, when the orgasm started to fade away, she opened her eyes, and scanned the cramped room with its paper towels, and stepladder, and boxes full of supplies for The

Panting Dog.

The sight of them was a gut check, and reality slammed into her. She'd gone and had sex in the storage closet of the bar she managed. During *her* party.

Her head felt cloudy, her body dizzy. But not from the pleasure. From the stark realization of what she'd done. She'd had sex with Smith to get him out of her system, and in doing so she'd broken a cardinal rule. She didn't sleep with her friends, and she sure as hell didn't get physical with men she could never be serious with.

Smith zipped his jeans, looking sexy and dreamy and precisely like the kind of man she'd hate herself for falling for.

"Come back to my house," he said in that voice that threatened to lure her yet again. From his delicious accent to his filthy words, he was some kind of drug. If she took another hit, she'd be addicted. He absolutely, positively had to be a one-time-only occasion.

She grabbed her panties from the floor, balled them up in her hand, and scrambled for an excuse, neurons now tripping over themselves as she plotted the fastest course out of her embarrassment. Her mind raced through plausible reasons to get the hell out of there. Headache? No, too typical. Forgot a morning appointment? No, that required too much explanation. She wanted to curse herself for not having a dog. Dogs were a perfect excuse because they needed to be walked.

Wait. She *did* know someone who had a dog.

"I can't. I'm dog sitting for Diane. I need to go walk Henrietta. Thanks for a fun night," she said.

She gave him a peck on the cheek, because that would

make her seem cool and unflustered, surely. She didn't look back when she opened the door to the storage room, grabbed her purse from the shelf where she'd left it earlier, stuffed her underwear inside, and hightailed it out the back door.

Once outside, she pressed her palm against the brick wall, needing to root herself to the real world again, not a fantasy one fueled by foolish lust. The warm night air rushed over her and the stars twinkled overhead, as she breathed in and out, each breath recalibrating and reminding her that she wasn't that kind of woman. She didn't do that kind of thing.

At least, she didn't plan to again.

She raced home, the whole time running through her to-do list for tomorrow, the next day, the rest of the week, the rest of her life. Anything to get tonight out of her mind.

Chapter Four

Jamie dropped her ereader in her purse, then added her migraine pills. She stopped at a framed photo she kept on her bureau. It was a picture of the dog and cat she'd had when she was younger. A handsome German shepherd her parents had named Tennyson, alongside their Siamese cat, Lord. Tennyson had been the best dog ever, loyal and devoted, and a complete sweetheart, especially considering how well he'd played with Lord.

If only she could find another German shepherd. But the breed was hard to come by at animal shelters. She'd tracked down a young puppy in a San Jose shelter last week, but was on a waiting list for him. She hadn't heard back, so she figured the puppy had gone to another home. She'd just keep checking with more local rescues until another puppy arrived.

A dog would surely take her mind off a certain someone. She repositioned the photo. Then moved it to the other end of the bureau. Or maybe it would look better in the middle. She'd already dusted, swept her floors, and scrubbed clean her kitchen counters. Her whole house was spotless, but her brain kept returning to last night.

"Crud," she muttered. She was stalling, and she knew it. She had to go to work in thirty minutes, and Smith would likely be there, working on the construction of the same back room where they'd danced. She'd avoided him today, his calls and his texts wanting to know if she was okay. But she'd have to man up in a few minutes, and what was she supposed to say?

Hey, you're a swell pal, and you screw like a rock star, but let's just pretend last night never happened, shall we?

Ugh.

The person she really wanted to avoid, though, was herself.

She couldn't believe she'd had sex with Smith, let alone *liked* that filthy mouth of his. She was a romantic. She had a soft spot for poems and wine and the finer things in life, so how the hell did she get off on a man who liked it down and dirty? He'd sent her into such a heated state, she was barely herself last night. She'd been pulsing, alive and trembling with want. She was supposed to fall for someone classy, who courted her with odes and stanzas, not hot, bossy words as he pinned her to the wall.

She dropped her head into her hand. What was wrong with her? She wasn't into that kind of rough play, she didn't need to be bitten, or manhandled, or talked to like that. But then, maybe she did, because those orgasms he delivered were the stuff you didn't just write a poem about; those were the kind of Os that made you write an anthemic album that sold millions of copies as everyone screwed and made babies to it.

She waved her hands in front of her face, as if she could wave off the memories of the Best. Sex. Of. Her. Life.

She marched into her living room, grabbed a book of Shakespeare's sonnets and sent a quick prayer to the Bard that he would reset her as the romantic she knew she was. God knew, the novel she'd tried reading this morning hadn't helped—she'd downloaded a racy romance about two coworkers who agree to a no-strings-attached relationship for one week, hoping that will cure them of the simmering lust they have for each other. Whether their tactic worked was up for debate—she'd had to set the story down when the hero pushed all the papers off the desk and lifted the heroine onto it. She'd been getting too hot and bothered for her own good.

Settling into Sonnet 116, she reacquainted herself with a reminder of the importance of having something in common with a partner. "Love is not love which alters when it alteration finds," she read out loud, nodding vigorously. Shakespeare was right. She and Smith were too far off the mark; they'd simply never work. Now take her parents—they were two like-minded people. They ran a winery together, they both loved wine and poetry, they liked the same books and movies, they were neat and orderly and they'd lasted through the years. On the other hand, there was Diane and the Douche. Her sweet sister went for the guy she was friends with, the life of the party type, and wound up being saddled with a divorce after only three years.

The proof was in front of her in her very own family. Smith would never be the kind of guy who could take care of a woman outside the bedroom. Though as soon as that thought touched down in her head, she flashed back to the Spring Festival last year. They'd played a few rounds of Skee-Ball, both their competitive spirits running strong. She'd won twice, he'd won twice, and they'd shared beers afterward. But then a cruel migraine had set in quickly. He walked her home, fixed her a quick cup of the green tea that sometimes took the edge off her headaches, then tucked her in bed and turned out the lights so she could sleep her headache away. She'd hate to lose that sort of closeness if anything else continued with them.

She slammed the book of poems shut. They weren't helping her forget him. She grabbed her phone and called her good friend Megan, who'd been living in LA for the last year. They'd gone to high school together, and Megan always gave solid advice. Her friend answered on the second ring, but didn't speak right away. Jamie was greeted instead by loud clang, then a frenzied "Hello?"

"Hey Megster, how's it going? You rearranging the furniture or something?"

"A pot just fell off the stove."

"I hope it wasn't boiling," Jamie said with a laugh.

"It wasn't. And it didn't actually fall. I bumped into it," Megan admitted sheepishly.

"You've always been prone to bumping into things."

"So true. What's going on up there? I miss you," she said with a wistful tone in her voice.

Jamie started to tell her about last night, but something stopped her. She didn't know what to say, or frankly, *why* she needed to talk about it. She'd already decided Smith was a one-time-only thing, so there was no need to rehash him.

Chin up, move on, keep on keeping on.

"You should come back to Hidden Oaks then," she said, shifting gears away from last night.

"I've been thinking about it. Things with Jason suck."

"Oh no. I'm so sorry. Is it more of the same?" She asked carefully because last she heard, Megan's boyfriend had been hitting the bottle a few too many times.

"Yeah. I never see him anymore. All he cares about is partying. I swear, I don't know what I ever saw in him or why I moved here. We have nothing in common," Megan said, frustration etched in her words. Jamie wanted to reach out and hug her, and tell her that somehow it was all going to work out. Not with Jason, but in general. They chatted some more, and Jamie checked her watch, realizing she needed to head to work.

"Okay, sweets. Call me if you need to talk more," she said, and even though they hadn't chatted about Smith, somehow she felt better for that. Maybe this was the clear evidence that she wasn't thinking about him—she didn't need to discuss him.

She slipped her bag over her shoulder, locked the door, and walked to work, several blocks from her small bungalow. She wore a jean skirt, a short-sleeve top, and ankle boots on her bare legs, the perfect ensemble for the warm spring day.

She walked past the local hair salon and the coffee shop, spotting a familiar face up ahead. Cara was walking her adorable black and white border collie mix in a perfect heel by her side. She was the best dog trainer in town, with a client list who adored her. Including Jamie's sister.

She was about to say hello, when she remembered that Smith had once dated Cara. But who cared? She wasn't dating Smith, and she certainly wasn't so petty that she wouldn't say hello for that reason. Besides, she was a dog person through and through, and she wanted to say hello to the pooch too.

"Hey Cara," she called out with a wave. "How's Violet?"

"She is excellent. A good girl as always," Cara said, and Violet sat by her owner's side as soon as Cara stopped walking.

Jamie bent down to pet the collie mix. The dog lifted her snout, giving her more room to scratch between her ears. "She's so cute," she said.

"How's Henrietta? Is she keeping Diane good company?"

A flush crept across her cheeks again as she remembered her excuse last night. But she sucked down her embarrassment. "She's the best dog."

"Diane said you were thinking about getting a puppy. A German shepherd?"

Jamie nodded. "If I can find one. I've been looking for one in a rescue. I'm on a waiting list."

"I'll keep my eyes open for you. They're good dogs."

"Thanks for doing that. I better get going into work. Don't want to be late," she said.

"See you around."

"You too," Jamie said with a cheerful wave. As she walked off, she was ready to pat herself on the back. She truly must have gotten Smith out of her system if it didn't bother her to run into an ex. Her plan had worked and had cured her of all her feelings for him.

Jamie held her head up high as she walked into the bar, ready to focus on work and prep for the wine tasting she was hosting in an hour.

"Hey, Jamie."

She was greeted by Becker—tall, broad, brooding, and the owner of the bar. He was with the fire department too, running the volunteer force. She was grateful to have a boss like Becker. He was a cool guy, only a few years older than her twenty-six years. Even though the bar was a microbrewery, he let her bring in some of her favorite wines for the grape lovers who flocked to town, and she'd also urged him to throw the kickoff party for the festival. He was eager to make his mark in town, and since she knew this town inside and out, he'd often turned to her for input on how to grow and expand the bar's presence. "So what's the verdict? How was the party you convinced me to have?"

"It went so well. Everyone had a good time," she offered with a cheery smile, forcing her brain to stay focused on the party itself, not what happened in the back of the bar as the event was winding down.

"Glad to hear that," he said, then asked with a wry smile, "Are you going to convince me to throw a party every month now?"

"I just might do that," she said. "But I do appreciate you letting me weigh in on things around here."

"Speaking of that, I have a meeting this evening. Talking to some of the other business owners on the town square. See how we can make the Spring Festival a success. If you have any ideas I'd love to hear them."

Her eyes lit up. She was glad to be able to contribute, and she admired that Becker was so focused on business. He worked late, he worked early, he worked a lot, and his brain was always ticking. She respected that about him.

"More games," she offered.

"More games?"

"Well, everyone loves to play Skee-Ball or Whac-A-Mole, so we just have to make sure we have as many of those options as possible."

"Whac-A-Mole," he said with a straight face, as he wrote something in a notebook. Was he writing down Whac-A-Mole? Becker really did take *serious* to new levels. That kind of discipline was admirable. "Got it."

"I'll think of some others as I'm prepping. We've got a wine tasting soon. I need to grab some bottles, but I'll have on my thinking cap."

"Great. Can't wait."

She stopped in the tiny office, dropped her purse on the chair, and then headed to the wine racks to consider the best selection. She was reaching for a pinot noir that had been raved about recently when she heard the back door open.

She swiveled around. There was Smith, carrying a toolbox in one hand and a stack of wood planks on his shoulder. The way he held the boards made his white T-shirt rise up, revealing smooth, tanned skin and muscles she'd run her fingernails over the night before. *Why* did he have to have abs she wanted to lick and pinch and bite?

Oh, right. Because he was the fireman women drooled over. He was the very reason there were fireman calendars, and fireman erotica, and let's face it, fireman fantasies.

And she was having one right now. A red-hot one about him pinning her against the wall. Saying naughty things. Bringing her there again. Oh lord, what had happened to her? Evidently, last night hadn't cured her at all.

It had only fanned the flames of her desire, and she was a twisted knot of emotions right now—wanting to feel nothing, but feeling so much for him. He might not be relationship material, but he sure was good-in-the-sack material. She didn't want to risk her heart, but maybe there was a way to preserve it *and* satisfy these cravings. Rather than a one-night stand, perhaps she needed a one-week trip. Maybe that couple in her novel had the right idea. One week, no strings. And heck, with such a finite period of time, she could keep their friendship intact too.

First things first, though. Before she proposed something crazy—she was going to have to play it like he would. Be cool, be easy, be casual. Make it seem like last night was no big deal.

• • •

His shoulders tightened when he saw her.

"How's Henrietta?" he said sharply, biting out the question. He hadn't intended to sound harsh, not when he was also worried that he'd scared her off. But the fact was, he was annoyed too. Frustrated with the way she took off last night. He didn't like being left, and he certainly didn't enjoy being left after what they'd done. What they'd said. How they'd both admitted feelings for each other. To top it off, this damn construction job was taking longer than he'd wanted. Between her ditching him and the possibility of falling behind schedule, he wasn't in his finest mood.

"Well?" he asked again, lowering the wood and the toolbox to the unfinished concrete floor. "Is she okay? Because I saw her on my drive home last night having a nice late-night walk with your sister."

Jamie swallowed and blinked. She tightened her hold on the bottle of wine, then finally met his gaze. But said nothing.

"You didn't have to walk Henrietta," he said, staring hard at her. Waiting for a reply. He held his hands out wide.

"I know," she said, looking at her feet.

"So you lied. What was that about? You just took off."

"Yeah. What of it?" she said with a steely-eyed coolness.

Whoa. This wasn't the Jamie he knew. Something was wrong. Something was off. Jamie was feisty, Jamie was sassy, but Jamie was never blasé. Jamie *always* cared. About everything from her job to her family to beating his ass in bowling when she could.

Then it hit him. She regretted it. Whether because their night had tarnished their friendship, or because he'd come on too strong with his rough ways and his dirty mouth, when he should have started more slowly with her, taken his time. He had to rein in his annoyance over last night and over work and smooth things out with her. Say he was sorry for taking her against the wall, instead of taking her out to a candlelight dinner and wooing her properly.

He walked over to her, letting go of the anger over her lying about the dog. He needed to reassure her. They stood inches away in the middle of the room. It was late afternoon, but the lights hadn't been installed in this section of the bar yet, so there were shadows across the two of them. "I thought we were having a good time. Hell, I know I was, and you sure seemed to be too. So will you need to take off again if I ask you out on a date?"

Her mouth dropped open. She stared at him as if he were speaking Swahili.

"A date," he continued. "That thing where two people who like each other spend more time together. You've heard of it?"

"What kind of a date?"

"Something you'd like. I can take you out to dinner. We can go to a bookstore and browse if you want," he said, trying hard to latch onto something that would win her over. Her lips quirked up as he asked her, but then she quickly reined it in and fixed her mouth in a straight, impassive line.

"I don't know if we should date, per se," she said, then let her voice trail off, and there was something almost suggestive in her tone. As if she were inviting him in for more. But he didn't want to read her the wrong way. So rather than assume, he decided to be direct.

He reached out and brushed a strand of blond hair away from her neck, trying for softness. He'd scanned through a few romance novels on his smartphone last night; the heroes were always brushing hair off a woman's face, neck, or shoulder. Maybe emulating those sensitive dudes would help him. "I'm sorry. Was I too rough?"

She tilted her head and shot him a questioning look. "Too rough?"

"I should have been gentler, right?" He was damn near ready to kick himself for letting his dirty thoughts get the better of him last night. He wished he could rewind the last twenty-four hours and try again with her. Court her properly, like a gentleman. He'd never been good with sweet words—love and romance. He certainly hadn't seen that from his parents—more like vitriol when they'd split, though he'd tried hard to keep them together.

Nor did sweetness fit his life these days. Fighting fires, tending to drunk driving accidents, as well as his regular construction job—well, they weren't conducive to bringing out the poet in him. Teasing, joking—those were easier ways to deal. When it came to women, he was much better off when he didn't try to be the sweet, sensitive guy.

But he was going to have to work harder for her. "You don't want to try again? Give us another chance? Because I thought we were pretty good together last night when we were making love," he said, hoping using sweeter words might work on her.

A smile danced across her lips again. "We were," she said.

Okay, so they were getting somewhere. "I'm so glad you agree," he said running his hand down her bare arm, and enjoying the way she shivered in response. "Do you want to try again?"

"It's just I thought we could try something else," she said, and she seemed to be taking her time, trying to figure out exactly what to say.

He was dying to know what she wanted to try, so he jumped at the invitation. "Try what?"

She was about to answer when Becker walked in. "Jamie, your sister's here. And she seems kind of upset."

The look in her eyes changed in a nanosecond to one of deep concern. He swore he could hear her heart beat fast, and the worry pound through her veins as she swiveled around, looking for her sister. He understood needing to talk to someone when times were tough; he hadn't had that luxury when he was younger and watched his parents' marriage sever. He had to give her some space.

Jamie turned to him and started to explain. "My sister. Her divorce has been hard on her."

"Yeah, I know. That sucks," he said, and smiled sympathetically. Whatever she wanted to try needed to be tabled. He knew her sister had to come first. "Go talk to her. She needs you."

Chapter Five

Asking Smith to have a no-strings-attached affair was like trying to speak underwater. She couldn't get the words out clear. She'd barely been able to manage the word *try*. But she shoved all thoughts of him aside for the time being.

"Tell me what's going on."

She pulled out a chair for her sister at the table in the back alley near a small oak tree. Diane plopped down in it, her shoulders sinking. Jamie's heart ached for her sister and all Diane had been through in the last year. Her ex had put her through hell and back.

Diane shook her head and sniffled. Jamie reached into her pocket for a tissue, handing her one.

Diane wiped her eyes. "I'm so glad you're such a nut about carrying tissues everywhere you go," she teased.

"You know me. I like to be prepared for anything," she said, because you simply never knew when you might need one. What if a public restroom, for instance, had run out of toilet paper? What if it was windy out and your eyes watered? Or what if someone you cared about needed to shed a few tears?

Diane blew her nose, a loud honking sound. "I found out there were more women," she said through broken sobs, and Jamie rubbed her back as she cried. It was supposed to be the other way around. An older sister taking care of a younger one. But, in their case, Diane was the one hurting. She then went on to detail the affairs she'd just learned of—apparently he'd been messing around with someone he used to visit during his shifts at the firehouse, among other extracurricular conquests. "But here's the worst part. He screwed my favorite barista at the coffee shop down the road. Do you have any idea how hard it is to find a good latte? And now, thanks to my ex, I need to search for a new coffee shop."

She was trying so hard to protect herself with anger, but Jamie knew how much this really did hurt. And not because Diane had placed the café on her blackball list, and with good reason. But because each new revelation of her ex-husband's infidelity must have made her feel like her already-broken marriage was shattering yet again. Like being kicked in the gut when you're already down.

"Well, then I am just going to have to learn to how to make the perfect mocha."

"You'd do that for me, wouldn't you?"

"Of course. You know I'd do anything for you. I'll sign up for barista classes or get myself one of those fancy silver machines from Bed, Bath and Beyond this weekend just for you," she said, and that earned her a sliver of a smile.

"Well, here's the one thing I want you to do," Diane said,

back to the big sister role.

"What is that?"

"Don't make my mistakes, promise me?"

Jamie's heart sputtered, and she felt as if Diane's big sister radar was so sharp she knew what had happened last night. And while last night was only a fling, the warning was loud and clear. Only get involved with someone reliable, serious, steady. She glanced at her hands so she wouldn't have to make eye contact. What would her sister think of her if she knew what had happened with Smith? Worse, if she knew she'd been contemplating going there again with him just for sex?

"I mean it," Diane said, grabbing her hand and squeezing it. "Don't fall for someone because he's fun and friendly, like my ex. I was all hook, line, and sinker for that carefree, happy-go-lucky man, and now look at me. Only give your heart to someone you can depend on."

Jamie crossed her heart, the gesture as much for Diane as for herself. "I promise."

"I should let you get back to work now. And I need to stop by the winery to sign forms for the new employees. We just hired some part-timers and they're working out well," she said, referring to their parents' winery that she managed.

"That's great to hear. I'm glad it's all working out. Want me to come over later? I'll get some ice cream and we can watch *Anchorman* again," she said, since that was her sister's favorite movie, and she was pretty sure Diane needed a Will Ferrell–induced laugh tonight.

"Yeah. That would be great."

Anchorman would help Jamie keep her mind where it belonged, too. Smith might be thoughtful, he might be fun to play Skee-Ball with, and he certainly could deliver mind-shattering orgasms, but he was also a recipe for late-night cries in a tub of ice cream.

• • •

What a difference the last twenty-four hours had made.

Her sister was feeling a smidge better from the double comfort of Ron Burgundy and Ben & Jerry's, and Jamie spent the next morning rereading some of her favorite Robert Browning poems to recalibrate her heart. Because she wanted a relationship like poetry, like her parents had. She was heading over to their house on Pine Crescent Road later this week for a regular dinner. Her sister and niece would be there, too. A nice family gathering, one where they all turned off their cell phones and were present in the moment.

Now, she walked from her little house to the nearby town square to pop into the local bookstore. She was an ereader gal, but she also loved the feel and smell of real pages for poetry and for children's stories, so she was a regular at An Open Book, directly across the wide grassy square where the festival would be held. She passed The Panting Dog, spotting Smith's truck a block ahead, a flashy silver number with the name of his construction company in bright red. He'd mentioned his business was booming and that he needed to expand. She wondered if he'd gotten around to finding help yet.

She headed straight for the kids' section to grab the newest Skippy Jon Jones picture book as a gift for her niece.

After she paid for the book, she spotted Smith...in the

frigging kids' section of the bookstore? She stopped in her tracks and knitted her brow, as perplexed as if she'd just seen him walking on his hands through the town square. "Um, hi?"

He swiveled around and flashed that all-too-familiar grin. His hands were full, and she didn't even pretend not to look. She raked her eyes over the bookstore bounty—Mad Libs.

"Something to keep you busy at the firehouse on a quiet night?"

"It's for the Burn Center, actually."

Her cheeks burned. "I'm sorry. I didn't mean to make light of your volunteer work. I think it's amazing that you give them so much time."

"I'm not offended. I like Mad Libs," he said, and she had to fight back a smile. Because—*Mad Libs*. That was adorable.

"What do you do when you volunteer?"

He'd once told her that was why the calendar mattered to him so much. As a fireman, he'd seen firsthand why a hospital needed a burn center, and all the proceeds from the calendar went to support it. But she didn't know the specifics of his volunteer work.

"I do Mad Libs," he said with a straight face. "With the kids. Some of the other patients, too. Often helps take their minds off what's going on. And let me tell you something. Use monkey as much as you can in a Mad Lib and you get everyone laughing."

"I can picture that perfectly," she said, and the image was a nice one. She was willing to bet that Smith had a way of making the patients forget about their woes for a while.

She could see him, kicking back in a blue vinyl hospital chair, reading off silly stories made by inserting nouns, verbs, and kinds of animals in the most random ways. He had the right disposition for that—someone who didn't take himself too seriously could be perfect to help kids feel better.

"But that's not the only reason I'm here," he said.

"Oh yeah? What's the other reason?"

"I bought you a gift. To say I'm sorry."

What on earth did he have to apologize for? She was the one who'd walked off. Stormed off, actually.

He showed her a small hardback book of poems on the top of the shelf where they stood. "I picked it up before I came over to this section. Maybe you have it already, but I know you like your poems, and well"—he stopped, looked down at the white and red book, and then back at her—"you probably already have Shakespeare's sonnets, huh?"

Her heart fluttered, and her hand flew to her chest. She hadn't expected this from him, neither the Mad Libs nor the gift. But she found she liked both. *A lot.* Maybe her idea would work after all. Besides, he'd been volunteering at the Burn Center for as long as she'd known him, and for the first time, she realized this showed something about him she'd never given him credit for—he could remain committed. That didn't mean she was ready to sign up for a long-term deal, but it made her feel better about her plan for a week-long tryst.

"For me?" she asked, wanting her nerves to stop skipping with some kind of high school excitement, but damn, she was about to cartwheel. He'd given her a gift, and she'd been... well, she hadn't been straight with him about anything.

"I wanted to say sorry for coming on so strong the

other night. I shouldn't have been so…well, I should have just asked you out on a date first, but then I did and you turned me down," he said, and forced out a laugh. "And I just don't want to lose you as a friend, so think of this as a peace offering, and I hope Shakespeare's words will be enough for you to forgive all those dirty things I said to you since I know you prefer poetry and roses."

When he handed her the book of sonnets, she grabbed onto his hand, not letting go. She had to be honest with him. They were friends, and it was the least she could do. She gulped, then looked him square in the eyes. "I love Shakespeare's sonnets, so thank you. I was actually reading them the other day, and they're beautiful. But that's not the reason I said I wanted to try something else."

He looked at her quizzically. "It's not?"

A young boy raced into the kids section and began pulling Captain Underpants books off the shelves with reckless glee, so Jamie motioned for Smith to join her in a quieter section by the shelves with the less-popular books on philosophy, set back from the rest of the store.

Then she blurted it out.

"I loved the dirty talk. And I loved the biting, even though I never thought I would. And I loved it against the wall," she said, her cheeks painted a bright red from serving up all those things she never thought she'd say, let alone like. But she owed him the full truth. "But we can't be involved, because let's call a spade a spade. You've never been into relationships. You're more the dating type, rather than the serious type. Besides, we're good friends, and I want us to stay that way, and that's why I want to propose something else. How about we have a no-strings attached sex-only deal for the next week?"

Chapter Six

His jaw hung open.

His brain was a pinball machine, lights and noises whirring in overdrive. He was half thrilled and half annoyed. Half turned on and half frustrated. This woman was throwing him off his game.

"Shit, I thought you were gonna be pissed at me forever for saying filthy things."

"No," she said, laughing, then she dropped her voice further. "I don't even swear, but I can't begin to tell you how hot it was when you said all those things to me. I like that dirty mouth of yours. Go figure, and I would love to have more of it."

He tried to suppress a wicked grin, but he had no luck. Hell, this was good news on the one hand. He'd been so worried he'd ruined everything after getting physical with her that he was terrified their friendship was history. But knowing she liked it the same way was a *huge* turn-on. The only trouble was she still didn't want to go out with him. She didn't want to date him. She only wanted to sleep with him. "But if you liked it so much then why not give us a go?"

"Because I do like you as a friend, and I want to stay that way. And I also don't want to be one more name on a list of women you've dated. I mean, Lisa was all over you at the party. And then there's Cara, and she's super sweet, but still, you used to date her. And even when I was at my sister's I drove past Melody Olsen's house, and you used to go out with her too. There are reminders everywhere that you date a lot of women and never for more than a few months, or weeks, really."

Damn, that list sounded long when she rattled off the names. He was never serious with any of them, and evidently that was the big fat fucking hurdle in the way of him having a relationship with Jamie. But he wasn't some sort of career playboy who needed or wanted a woman in every port. He simply hadn't met the right woman. "I'm not going to lie to you and act like I'm some goody-goody choir boy. I'm not. I'm not a monk," he said. "But I'm not going to pretend you aren't one hundred percent special to me either. I like you a lot. I have a good time with you. I laugh with you. Hell, we've gone bowling together for a couple years now, and I just think that's gotta count for something," he said, and shot her what he hoped was a sexy grin that might melt her.

"See, that's the other thing. I don't want to be a 'count for something' kind of thing. I don't want to be a 'why not' woman—"

He cut her off. "I didn't mean it like that. I didn't mean to imply *let's go out because there's nothing better.* You're not a 'why not' kind of woman. I swear. That's why I want to take you out and spend time with you. You can even invite me over to your sister's house for your dinners and I'll happily go. I want more."

Her eyes widened with shock at the suggestion. She looked mortified that he'd want to have dinner with her family. She lowered her voice and motioned for him to come closer. "I know I wasn't up-front when I ran out the other night, but I'm going to be blunt now. That was *the* best sex of my life," she said, and pride burst through him with the compliment. She continued, "Plus, you're funny, and you're sweet, and you make me laugh, and I care deeply for you as a friend, and that's why I want to be friends with benefits for a week," she said, then raised her eyebrows playfully. "You like the benefits part, don't you?"

He gritted his teeth and felt his shoulders tighten with frustration. She was calling him out but yet she still wanted to sleep with him?

Then it hit him. *She wanted to sleep with him.* She wanted to have sex with him, no-strings attached, for a week. He could work with that. She said he was the best sex of her life, and if he was going to have to use sex to win her heart, then dammit, he'd do that. Play to his strengths. Make her feel everything, and in doing so, make her fall for the rest of him. Rather than be offended with her proposition, he was going to run with it and ensure at the end of the week, she would want all of him.

He would have to prove himself to her, and that was part and parcel of what was so damn attractive about her. He was used to getting what he wanted. He wasn't being cocky, just honest. He had friends, he had steady work, he had good health, and he had women when he wanted them.

But there was something about having to step outside of his comfort zone that he now craved, and Jamie was the first who'd called him on his ways. He had to shed his defenses for her. Not always his first choice, but it was the only choice with her, and it was one he was willing to make.

"I can do this, but there's one thing I want out of the deal."

"Besides sex?"

He nodded, inching closer to her, the corner of the bookshelves shielding them, as he lazily trailed his fingers down her bare arm. "You know we have fun together, and you know we fuck well, so let's go out once. As friends. A friends-with-benefits date."

"Smith," she said, but her voice was already breathy. Her eyes looked hazy as he touched her, telling him she was starting to bend.

"One date, as part of your no-strings-attached plan," he said, now reaching for her waist, brushing his fingers across her hipbone. She shivered at his touch, and he glanced around, glad they were in a section where no one could see where his hands were daring to travel. "Let me take you out to dinner at the end of the week on a proper date," he said in a low voice, as he played with the waistband of her skirt. She drew a sharp breath.

"Maybe," she said, and her eyes started to flutter shut.

He moved closer and shifted her body. Her chest faced the shelves, so no one could see what he was doing as he stood behind her, grazing his hands underneath her shirt, then across her belly. "We could see a movie. Or we could have dinner and as we wait for the food, I could tell you about all the ways I want to take you again," he said.

She arched her back against him. "Yeah?"

"And then after dinner, when you're squirming under the table, all hot and bothered and as amped up as I am, you can come back to my place, and I can fuck you senseless on the kitchen table, or up against the wall, or maybe just in the hallway because we'll want each other so badly we can't make it to the bedroom," he said, his voice a low, dirty growl near her ear. "And it'll be what you want, no strings attached."

She hitched in her breath, not answering his question about a date. But right now, he wasn't thinking about her yes to dinner; he was thinking about making her scream *yes*. He brushed the hair away from her ear, his lips buzzing her earlobe. "Are you wet for me right now?"

She didn't answer with words. She merely nodded.

"Do you get wet for me when you're alone, Jamie?"

"Yes," she whispered, her shoulders rising and falling.

He yanked her hips back so her behind slammed into his erection, straining through his jeans. "I can picture you, sprawled out and naked, your hand between your legs. Have you ever gotten off to me?"

She reached her hand in the small of the space between their bodies, rubbing him through his jeans. Her fingers felt like electricity shooting through him, crackling sparks lighting up his blood and bones at her touch.

"Yes," she answered.

"I would love to see that. You on your bed, letting your legs fall open. I'd love to stand in your doorway, to find you in the dark. Your eyes are closed, your head thrown back, those pretty pink pussy lips wet and glistening for me."

She bit back a moan, and circled her ass against him, her

body starting to take over. He teased her more, tracing the edge of her panties with his fingers. "I'd watch you, and I'd have to touch myself because it'd be so fucking hot to see you like that, your finger rubbing your clit, your other hand squeezing your breast as you touch yourself. Do you touch your breasts when you play with yourself?" he asked, hot in her ear, as she rubbed against him, her delicious ass making him feel like his dick was a steel rod.

"Sometimes," she said in a hot whisper.

"And then I bet you thrust those hips when you get closer, just like you're doing right now. You part your legs and start fucking your own hand hard, picturing my face between your legs. Is that what you fantasize about?"

"*Yes*," she said, her voice bordering on a desperate cry.

"I would love to be licking your pussy right now, and sucking on your sweet clit, and have you writhing and moaning, your hands grabbing for my hair, pulling my face to you."

"Oh my," she gasped, as he dragged his hand between her legs, cupping her through her damp panties. She dropped her head back onto his shoulder. "I can't take it. I need you now."

Yes, he wanted to pump his fist. Only ten minutes into their new arrangement and things were working. He was going to win her over through sex. By giving her more of the best of her life and proving that he could be the man she wanted in the bedroom and out of the bedroom.

"Meet me outside," he told her, and she smoothed out her shirt and left the store, while he carried the books in front of him to hide his hard-on. He stopped by the register to quickly pay for the Mad Libs, telling the bookstore owner to keep the change. They walked quickly around the block to his truck. He held the door open for her and watched as she scooted inside, his eyes roaming over her sexy body, her bare legs, her face rosy with lust.

He hopped into the driver's side and turned on the ignition. "Where to?"

"I can't wait much longer. Just pull over on Circle Street," she said, gesturing ahead of them to a dead-end street. Twilight had set in, and he pulled over on the side of the road. She unbuckled her seat belt and launched herself at him, her hair spilling over his chest as she grabbed his face for a rough kiss.

His kind of kiss. The kind that could leave marks.

"Condom," she rasped out, breaking the kiss.

He reached into his wallet for one, then slid over to the passenger side. She unzipped his jeans and yanked them down to his knees. She tugged off her panties quickly and never had he ever been so grateful that a woman was wearing a skirt.

"You're gonna ride me hard now, got that?"

She nodded, her eyes wild with abandon. She looked like she could come within seconds, and it was a look she wore well.

"I am going to ride you so hard, Smith," she said with narrowed eyes and a bossy tone, like she was reveling in this newfound side of herself, this naughty side.

"That's right. I don't want you to slow down one bit," he said, as he rolled on the condom. In seconds, she climbed on him and sank down, taking him all the way in. Damn, she was so hot and tight, but he didn't have a chance to even savor that because she was fucking him hard, just like they both wanted.

She grabbed onto his shoulders and rode him like he was a pole, her sexy little body shooting up and down his cock, taking him deep with each thrust. Tremors rolled through him with each move she made. His blood flowed thick and heavy as he watched her, loving the way she let go like this. She was a different woman; she had a wild side that he'd somehow tapped into, and the thought that she saved it just for him fueled him.

She started panting and moaning, letting go now that they were in his truck. She rose up then back down on him, taking him all the way inside her. Pleasure rippled through his veins.

"That's right. Keep fucking me. Fuck me till your legs shake and you can't walk straight," he instructed, feeling his own orgasm within sight. "I want you to come so loudly that the neighbors will know how good I make you feel."

"You make me feel so good," she said, her breathing labored and erratic, her gorgeous face wracked with pleasure. He watched as she bit down hard on her lip, squeezing her eyes shut as she lowered herself down on him again. He felt her clench and tighten around him, her wet heat grabbing his cock as she started to shudder, then cried out loudly, shouting his name. The sound of her moans was his undoing, and his own orgasm tore through his body as he jerked against her, heat flooding through his veins as he came. She fell against him, her chest slumped onto his, as his cock twitched inside her, their harsh session on the side of the road starting to subside.

He pulled out of her and she handed him a tissue for the condom. "I'll throw this out later," he said, with a wink as he stuffed it into a trash bag in the car. "By the way, you look beautiful all the time, and you look especially beautiful when you come," he whispered. He ran his fingers softly through her hair, as she rested against his chest, looking thoroughly sated.

She shivered at his touch. "I do?"

"You do. Gorgeous and sexy and unbelievably hot and I love knowing I did that to you."

"You bring out this crazy side of me," she said, with an almost embarrassed grin.

He brushed his thumb across her lips. "It's not crazy. It's part of you. And I'm glad you share it with me," he whispered tenderly, then kissed her throat. She stretched her neck, giving him more access to work his way up to her ear, as he buzzed his lips against her skin. "And I'm going to show you the other sides of me," he said.

"Hmmm," she said in a dreamy, after-sex voice.

"Is that a yes to a dinner date at the end of the week?"

"I don't know what it is. All I know is I like this side of you a heck of a lot," she said, then looped her arms around his neck. Soon, she was brushing soft, sweet kisses against his jawline, and they felt a little bit like the start of real affection, not just lust. She slid off him and readjusted her clothes and he buttoned up his jeans.

She reached for the book of poetry he'd bought her. "Want to hear my favorite poem?"

"I would love to," he said, and then listened carefully as she read him a sonnet.

She turned to him when she was done, her eyes wide and brimming with hopefulness, as if she truly wanted him to like the words. "What do you think?"

"I'm not going to claim it makes a hell of a lot of sense to me, but I think Shakespeare had a way with words, and I like listening to you read it. Now, want to play Mad Libs with me?"

She laughed and nodded, then stretched her legs across him.

"Here's the thing," he said. "You need to use your fancy lyrical words, okay?"

She saluted him. "I'm up for it."

They played Mad Libs in the front seat of his car, combining Shakespeare with silliness, as he made her laugh, and she made him smile, until he needed to return to work. He'd been hoping to have a night off—go to the gym, play hoops with some of the guys from the firehouse. But that wasn't an option—the bar project was taking longer than he'd expected, and he had no one else to call on to shoulder some of the load.

"I should go. That back section of the bar isn't going to build itself," he said, trying to keep the frustration that nagged at him at bay.

"You think it'll be done soon?" she asked.

"Why? You hoping to have me out of your hair and not run into me in the back of the bar?" he said, making light of the situation.

She pushed back on his shoulder gently with her hand, not giving in to his attempts. "No. Because you sounded annoyed that you have to work tonight. Are you?"

He shrugged because the truth was he didn't really want to start talking about work. He just wanted to finish the damn job for Becker. Last thing he needed was to have his friend ticked off at how long it was taking. If he had to stay up all night he would. He'd gotten a call earlier in the day about building a new sundeck onto a house in the hills. He was going to have to find time to squeeze that in too. "Nah, it's not a big deal," he said, waving off her concerns.

"Smith," she said gently, fixing him a serious stare. "Do you need help with it?"

"You offering to take up a hammer and nails? Maybe get a little construction belt? You'd look mighty hot in some work boots, cut-off shorts, and a little tool belt around your waist."

She rolled her eyes. "You always make light of things."

He didn't have an answer, because she was right.

"But seriously," she said, persisting. "You're going to wear yourself out. You should hire help."

"I'm fine. I can do it myself. I've got it under control," he said, because he didn't want to talk about work or the things that weighed on him, so he did what she asked him to do—focus on sex.

"Hey, since you seem to like me for my body, what would you say to another round tonight? I can come by after I finish up my work tonight?"

"Now you're getting the hang of our deal," she said as she ran a hand across his thigh.

"Darlin', I got the hang of our deal when you were screaming my name at the top of your lungs."

She blushed, but grinned wickedly and moved in for another kiss, erasing all thoughts of business and work and the way he'd have to spend his evening. None of that mattered because he'd have more of her at the end of the night. But the next day, he'd need to start focusing on winning not just her body, but her heart. He had seven days to woo her.

Chapter Seven

Smith rested his elbow on the rolled-down window of his truck as he returned to the fire station. He'd been to the grocery store, picking up food for the next shift, and had about thirty minutes left before quitting time. It had been a long twenty-four hours with a handful of car accidents to tend to. No major injuries, though, and he was grateful for that.

His mind rolled back to Jamie once more, returning to the bookstore and truck encounter earlier in the week, as well as the last few nights they'd spent enjoying each other's bodies. She'd stopped by his house every night he wasn't working, and those were the best parts of the day—the moments with her, alone in his bedroom, in the living room, even the kitchen counter, as they drove each other to new heights of pleasure. All the images were burned brilliantly in his brain. But he couldn't rest on their chemistry. He needed to plan a fantastic date for Jamie. To show her he could give her more than just pleasure. That he was the man she could trust and depend on, like she wanted and needed.

He pulled into the fire station and cut the engine. He pushed thoughts of Jamie aside when he saw the guys starting to ready the quint. Fires were rare in Hidden Oaks, so based on the speed of the prep—leisurely—chances were good the quint was for some kind of minor incident.

"What's the story?" Smith asked as he shut the door and carried in the groceries.

His buddy Travis strolled toward him, his low-key stride making it clear they weren't prepping for a five-alarm anything. He pulled a quarter from his pocket, so Smith knew what was coming next. "I'll tell you, but first—heads you win, tails you lose."

Smith was never one to back down from a bet, even though he didn't know the stakes. "I'm in. What's it for?"

"If you can guess who just called. Here's your hint: Cat's stuck in a tree on Pine Crescent Road."

Smith groaned as he put away the food in the fridge and cupboards. "Not again?"

"Yup. Again."

"Never in my twenty-eight years of life have I met a cat who cannot come down from a tree on his own. Except for Melody Olsen's."

Melody had asked him out two years ago. Then one year ago. Then a few months ago. He wasn't feeling it for her, so he'd said thanks but no thanks. She still liked to send him naughty text messages now and then. He ignored them all. He wasn't going to lead her on by answering them. Lately, though, she'd been finding inventive ways to get around his lack of response. This was the second time she'd called about her cat. Fine, her tabby was quite a tree climber. But still...

"She asked for you. She wants you to go get her pussycat," Travis said and then slapped his thigh.

"How long have you been waiting to make that joke, Trav?"

"Since we got that call five minutes ago." Travis flipped the coin in the air, catching it in one quick motion, then brandishing the tails side in his palm. "And tails says you're coming along."

But Smith waved him off. "Let me just run out there. Save you guys the hassle. That branch is maybe ten feet high and I've got my work ladder in my truck. It'll do."

"You know we gotta answer every call, no matter how ridiculous."

"I know. But it's a Friday night in wine country, and we don't all need to be off dealing with this in case something serious happens. I'm on my way home and I can take care of it."

Thirty minutes later, he handed a loudly meowing cat—who honestly looked a little pissed, almost as if he'd been parked up there in that branch—to Melody Olsen.

"Thank you so much. He's been there for hours, and I know he's been terrified," she said, as she stroked the black and silvery feline's head.

"He's all safe and sound now and barely nicked a nail."

Melody held her cat tight, then tipped her forehead to her house with its wraparound porch. She'd placed two empty wineglasses and a bottle on a table by the porch railing.

"You want to join Tiger and me for a glass of wine?" she said coyly, as she stroked the cat in what she likely thought was a seductive fashion. The petting did nothing but remind him of Jamie. And how he'd like her to be the one inviting him over. Have a drink with her on the porch—beer for him, wine for her—talk about their day, look at the stars. Hell, he'd even be up for a little poetry if she wanted that. She intrigued him to no end—she was tough on the outside, but had a real vulnerable side underneath that she showed him now and then. She'd laid it out for him at the bookstore, being honest and blunt about what she wanted in life and love—a reformed playboy.

He'd have to be that for her.

"Thank you, ma'am. But no, thank you. I'm just glad your boy's okay." He gave the cat a quick pet between the ears before sliding into his truck to return to the fire station.

He turned the engine on as Melody waved good-bye and then made the cat wave, too. He laughed and gave an imaginary tip of the hat to Tiger. That's when it hit him.

Cats and dogs.

Jamie loved animals. Dogs especially, and he had just the idea for her.

Not for a date, but something else.

It was a damn good thing Melody's cat had found his way up that tree branch again, after all. Feeling pretty pleased with himself, he turned up the radio in his car, blasting a Billy Currington tune and singing along as he bumped down Melody's long, gravelly driveway. He spotted Jamie's car heading down the street. Her parents lived on this stretch of road, too. He waved to her, but when she gave him a sharp-eyed stare, he cursed and smacked the wheel with one hand.

She was jumping to the wrong conclusion, and he wished he could hop out of his truck and explain that he'd been saving a pet and nothing more. But from the way Jamie glared at him—even from a distance—he knew she was thinking he'd been playing cat and mouse with Melody.

He scrambled to find his phone, but by the time he grabbed it and called her, it went straight to voicemail.

• • •

"I heard you and Smith were hanging out in the bookstore earlier in the week."

Jamie raised one eyebrow at her sister as they washed the sundae dishes in the kitchen while their parents played with Diane's daughter in the living room.

"Oh really?"

"Yeah, friend of mine was there. Said the two of you looked pretty flirty," Diane said playfully as she rinsed off chocolate syrup from a bowl.

Jamie concentrated on drying a plate, rubbing the towel over it several times so she wouldn't have to look at her sister. She didn't want to admit to anything, not after the promise she'd made, and certainly not after spotting Smith cavorting with that cat woman.

"Something going on with him?" Diane elbowed her.

"No."

She stared at her. "Honestly?"

"No," she said, but she didn't like lying to her sister. She sighed, then managed some of the truth. "Okay, we kissed at the kickoff party. That was all."

"You like him?"

"Yes," she admitted grudgingly, though the word was hard to get out because she'd never planned on feeling this way. "But who doesn't?"

"He's gorgeous. Be careful, though. You know what happened to me when I got involved with a friend."

"Don't worry. Nothing more is going to happen," she said, and that was the truth, the whole truth, and nothing but the truth. Though her heart hurt for the first time at the thought of nothing more.

"Why?" Diane asked, tilting her head and looking curiously at her sister.

"Why what?"

"Why is nothing more going to happen? You kissed him. You just said you liked him. I still think you need to be cautious, but that gets even harder when you like someone."

Like. Sure, she liked Smith. As a friend, as a buddy, as a friend with benefits, and he'd been giving her lots of benefits the last few days and nights. That man was masterful with her body and she found herself craving more and more of his naughty mouth. Truth be told, she'd enjoyed their chats after sex too—the conversations had been just as good as when they were friends-without-benefits. That was the trouble—she'd always been able to talk to him easily. They were starting to develop more of a connection—he made her laugh, he cared about her feelings, and he seemed to genuinely not want to hurt her.

But that was all, wasn't it? Jamie shrugged as if it were no big deal.

"Oh no. That's not how we do it," Diane said, poking her sister in the arm. "Do. You. Like Him? As more than friends?"

Jamie drew a deep breath, letting the air fill her body, hoping it would bring answers too. "Maybe?" she offered. "But I worry he's going to be like you-know-who."

"Listen, I'm not going to pretend to tell you that you can always trust someone forever and ever. But I know this much. Cara told me he was always nice to her when they went out. A total gentleman, and they're even still friends, but she broke up with him because she thought he always had eyes for someone else."

"Who?"

"She didn't say. But maybe the woman he really wanted is you, Jamie."

Her heart dared to skip a beat, and this time it wasn't just from lust. It was from hope.

Chapter Eight

Her cat was stuck in the tree.

The message glared at her when she turned her cell phone on as she got in her car. She jammed the key into the ignition, wanting desperately to believe him but knowing the risks and feeling duped nonetheless.

As she turned on the car, her phone flashed again.

She glanced at it and did a double take. *Meow — I really was in a tree. -Tiger.*

She fought back a silly grin with no success. She wanted to be angry, to curse him, but the text cracked her up. She grabbed the phone and called him back as she drove. Maybe Diane was right.

"Is anything on fire?"

"Nothing but my muscles and they're burning from working out hard," he said.

She laughed. "Are you at the gym?"

"Just finished," he said, and he sounded weary. "But now

I'm home and about to crash. Long day. Long shift. Twenty-four hour shifts do that to you."

"I can imagine. So the cat was in a tree? For real?" she asked, her voice still laced with skepticism. But it was a skepticism she wanted to shed.

"Swear on my life."

"You know that's the classic fireman cliché."

"But it's true."

She rolled her eyes even though he couldn't see her as she drove. "Look, I know this is no-strings-attached, but I need to know for sure that you aren't messing around with anyone else this week."

"I'm not, I promise," he said, and she could hear the earnestness in his tone, but she could also *feel* it, as if she were holding it in her grasp. "I wouldn't do that. I swear on my men, on all my guys at the firehouse. I swear on the way I'd protect them and run into burning houses to save a kid, a family, a dog, even a cat, that I was only there on a work call."

"You swear?" she asked, her voice trembling. At some point she was going to have to decide whether to let go of her fears. But she knew the word of the fireman was a true one.

"I swear. She had a bottle of wine, and she tried to get me to stay, but I left. I'm not interested in her. I am only interested in the gorgeous, smart, fiery woman I bought a book of poems for. Besides, you have to know me well enough by now to know that I'm not that kind of a guy. When I'm with a woman I'm with that woman, and you might have declared this 'no-strings attached' and that's fine for now, but my string is only attached to you."

Her heart thumped wildly, and she gripped the steering wheel so she could focus on the road. The sentiment was so sweet that it made her long for him. Besides, the truth was she did know him. And while he'd had a long line of ladies, maybe she'd been judging him simply for being lucky in love. She'd assumed that meant he strayed. But you could be lucky in love and be faithful. She decided right then and there to let go of all her lingering jealousy. She might not ever want more from him, but she wanted this thing they had—this fling—to be just between them. And part of that meant she needed to say good-bye to her worries about other women. Because they were just that—*her* worries. Nothing more.

"I do know you. I'm going to believe you."

"Good. You should," he said and yawned.

"Hard shift?"

"Yeah, there were a few car accidents we had to tend to."

"Anyone hurt badly?"

"Rushed a family over to the hospital but it was all minor bumps and bruises."

"That's scary but I'm glad it was okay."

"Me too," he said, taking another yawn. "Hey, was that our first fight as friends with benefits?"

She stopped at a light. "I think so."

"I like how it resolved."

"Me too." She paused and her mind rolled through an idea. Playfulness slinked back into her voice as she asked, "How tired are you?"

"I'm never too tired for *that*, if you're saying what I think you're saying."

· · ·

Ten minutes later, he opened the door and Jamie stood on his porch, the moonlight illuminating her. The faint glow of the half-light made her even prettier, her blond hair streaming down her back and over her shoulders. He was about to make a wisecrack about late-night visitors, but she pressed her lips against his in the sweetest kiss anyone had ever given him. In seconds, she'd disarmed him, and a groan escaped his throat. She brushed her lips lightly against his, kissing so softly it was as if she were barely there. But that's what made her kiss so enticing; it was a promise of more.

They stood like that kissing—only kissing—for minutes, and soon he threaded his hands into her hair, savoring the soft feel of the strands on his rough fingers.

"Hi," he said when she broke the kiss.

"Hi. I have a late-night delivery for you," she said, and trailed her hands down his shirt. His breath caught in his throat as her fingers danced across his stomach, and she smiled as she traced the outline of his abs. He grabbed her arms gently but firmly, and pulled her into the house.

"Whatever delivery you have for me I don't need the neighbors seeing," he said.

The door was swinging shut as she claimed his mouth again. She kissed harder this time, sliding her tongue across his, searching his mouth as she laced her fingers through his. It was as if she were claiming him, and he wanted that.

"I'm sorry I was worried about Melody," she said as she pulled away.

"Don't even think twice about it. I kind of like how you

want me all to yourself," he said, running his finger along her cheek.

"I do. And I want to do something for you."

He quirked an eyebrow in question.

"You've had a long shift. You work hard. And I want you to sleep well."

"What do you have in mind?" he said, but whatever it was he was sure he'd like it, judging from the way hot tension started to roll through his veins, especially when she wedged herself between his legs, rubbing against his erection. He grabbed her hips, tugging her closer.

She looped her hands around his waist. "You have the sexiest back," she said, and before he could respond, she'd dipped her hands below the waistband of his shorts, touching his bare ass. "Have I told you how much I love that you go commando?"

"You have not. Feel free to tell me now."

"It is so hot," she said, cupping his cheeks and squeezing. "You might have the best butt in the world."

"Ass. You can call it an ass," he teased, getting a kick out of how she still couldn't bring herself to swear.

"*Butt*," she said playfully, as she inched his shorts down to the ground.

She stood up and tugged off his shirt. She brushed her chest against him, sending a sharp hot jolt down his body. "Nice ass," she said, like it was the most forbidden thing she'd ever breathed.

"Very good," he said, and traced his finger across her lips. "I knew you had a dirty side. Now can I get you to say 'fuck me, Smith?'"

"No," she said, shaking her head coyly. "Because that's

not what we're doing. I have something else in mind." She brought her lips to his ear and whispered hotly, "I want your cock in my mouth."

For a second he was simply shocked. Then his body raced with desire, and he nearly burst inside as the naughty words from the woman he wanted rang in his head. "You *do* have it in you to be a dirty talker," he said appreciatively.

"Maybe you're growing on me," she said, as she wrapped a hand around him, and in an instant the talking ceased.

He couldn't speak. He could only curse—and groan—as she stroked him from the base all the way to the head, and he watched her the whole time. Her eyes were intense and full of lust. The look on her face was one he'd take a mental picture of to recall later. To have her touching him like this, like she wanted him this badly, was all he could ask for.

She dropped to her knees and kissed him.

Another moan escaped him as she surrounded him with her warm, wet mouth. The way she took him was both sweet and scorchingly hot at the same time. She looked like a goddess—*his* goddess—with her flowing blond hair, and that beautiful face, and those red lips locked tight as her tongue explored every inch of him.

He twined his hands into her hair. She moved faster, sucking him hard, and he could feel himself nearing the edge, electricity crackling through his veins.

He somehow found the Herculean strength to gently, but insistently, pull her away.

"What? You don't like it?"

He pulled her up, leveling her with his eyes. "I love it. I love watching you suck me off, Jamie. And I want nothing more than to fuck those pretty little lips of yours."

"So do it," she said in a sexy purr that sent his blood racing faster.

"I want to be inside you —" he started to say.

She shook her head and pressed her finger against his lips. "This is for you. I want to do this for you."

Before he could protest or try to take her the way he wanted, he let her give instead as she returned her lips to him. The temperature in his body rose precipitously as she sucked harder, taking him deeper. He grappled at her hair, grabbing hard and groaning as she worked her tongue and lips over him. Pleasure forked through his body. He took a deep, fueling breath, but soon his breathing grew stilted and his hips jerked as she sent him over the edge.

His shoulders shook from the aftershocks. When she stood up, wiping the back of her hand across her mouth, he tugged her in close. "Wow."

"I think that's the quietest you've even been."

"You took me by surprise," he said, petting her hair softly.

"Good. Now go get some rest," she said, then kissed him quickly on the cheek. "I'll see you tomorrow."

"Spend the night?" he asked, his voice rising a touch with hopefulness.

She shook her head. "Another time."

But time was running out, and soon their week would be over.

She left, the door falling shut behind her. As he drifted off, he was left completely satisfied but also thoroughly vexed, wondering if she would ever spend the night, and hoping to hell she would want more than just these benefits someday very soon.

Chapter Nine

When Jamie walked into The Panting Dog the next day, she was feeling pretty good. Their deal had been working out quite well, and the last few nights had been fantastic. He made her body sing, and last night, she'd been able to do something for him. She'd enjoyed giving without taking anything back for herself. He seemed to need it, and she was glad she was the one woman who would give it to him.

Becker was behind the bar, finishing up a phone call. Likely to a supplier, since he was discussing shipments and orders. She nodded a quick hello as she headed to her regular post, dropping her purse next to the iPad where she kept track of the wine sales.

She spotted a thick envelope taped to her iPad. Her name was on it, written in blocky letters. A man's handwriting, for sure, but what intrigued her was the simple sketch of a dog's paw next to her name. She slid a finger under the flap and opened the envelope.

Come to me in my dreams.

Her heart threatened to melt. It was a line from a Matthew Arnold poem, one she adored. Then, words from Smith.

These nights have been amazing. To "Another Time" very soon.

Okay, now a flock of butterflies swarmed her insides, turning her to mush. Damn him, with his double whammy of sweet words from a poet and sweet words from his own pen. Triple points for the dog paw since he knew she loved dogs. The grinding of a drill echoed through the bar, and, oddly enough, it thrilled her. Smith was here and she would be able to see him.

Wait. She wasn't supposed to want to see him for more than sex, so why was she so dang excited for the possibility of a few minutes with him? She didn't have time to contemplate, though, because Becker hung up and said a quick hello. He sounded frustrated.

"What's going on?" she asked.

He scrubbed his hand across his jaw. "Just want this construction to be over soon and get things back to regular around here."

"It has been a while, hasn't it?"

"It's taking longer than I thought," he said, reaching for a glass and filling it with water from the sink as the drilling ended, replaced by hammering.

Jamie winced; the sound of the hammer seemed to reverberate in her skull. She could feel a headache start to take root from the noise. "It is getting a little annoying."

"I know. What I would give for some silence in this place when the customers aren't here," Becker said, shaking his head and looking like a man longing for solitude. Odd that he'd chosen to run a bar when he seemed to crave quiet rather than crowds. But she wasn't going to play amateur shrink. Instead, she honed in on how she could help him with the matter at hand, because she wanted to keep proving her value as his manager. An idea started to form. She flashed back to something Diane said a few days ago about adding some new hires at the winery, and how they'd worked out well.

"Well, let's just move the project along then," she said to Becker, a cheery tone to her voice.

"How so?"

"Smith needs to hire some help and I know how he can do it," Jamie said, and marched to the unfinished section.

Smith's back was to her and he had on headphones, singing along to some country song as he hammered nails into the wood.

He could carry a tune, and she added that to his list of positive traits. Good voice, head full of poetry, sinful body. And his heart in the right place, from his volunteer work to the sweet way he'd looked out for her when Diane had showed up crying the other day—quickly giving her the space she needed to talk to her sister. She stopped in her tracks momentarily, letting her mind wander. She could imagine herself in his house, him maybe working on some fix-it project, her tiptoeing over after breakfast and softly running her fingers along his skin. He'd turn around, plant a devastating kiss on her mouth, then carry her up the stairs two by two to the bedroom.

Pin her down, hold her close, make love to her.

Oh, crap.

She could not start thinking of him that way. It was sex, only sex. They weren't making love, and certainly not in some imaginary house in her fantasies.

Because if it didn't work out—and of course it wouldn't work out—he'd eventually end it because they wanted different things—then she'd be saying sayonara to a friendship she didn't want to give up.

He hammered once more, and the sound crashed into her head, sending off a new pang. She pressed her hand to her forehead as Smith turned around. "You okay? You got one of those nasty migraines again?"

"Yeah," she said in a strained voice because it was coming on fast.

He reached for her shoulders, turning her around. He said nothing. Instead, he let his hands do the talking, his fingers kneading gently into her neck, then the dip of her shoulders. She sighed deeply and leaned into his touch. He lifted her hair so he could press his thumbs against the base of her scalp. The whole time, she moaned, but not the way she had in his truck or the storage room or his bedroom. The sounds came from relief, from the fact that he was taking away the pain, bringing her body back to the way it should be.

"You have magic hands," she said softly, as the tension poured out of her, replaced only by the soft, noodly feeling of a massage well done.

"You feeling better?"

She nodded into his hands.

"Don't stop, please."

"Never," he whispered, and she wasn't sure if he was even talking about the massage anymore. But she knew this much — she didn't want this thing between them to stop. Any of it. She inched her whole body closer as he moved on to her shoulders, rubbing her tight muscles between his fingers. Her back was nearly pressed against his chest, and she could feel his erection against her backside. She wriggled playfully against him once.

"You like that, too?" he asked.

"I like all the things you do," she whispered. "That's the problem."

"But it's not a problem. It doesn't have to be a problem if you just give me a chance," he said, and that idea was starting to grow on her. She didn't know how to admit it, though, so she stayed silent for now, as he kept up the work on her neck and shoulders, then moved his hands into her hair.

"I don't have a headache anymore."

"I'm so glad to hear that."

"You have no idea how much I needed this," she said, and it sounded as if her voice might break. "I've been dealing with these stupid tension headaches forever and nothing has made them go away like you." She snapped her fingers to demonstrate, then turned around to face him. "Thank you. Where did you learn how to do that?"

"I went to masseuse school. Didn't you know?"

She grinned, then swatted his chest playfully. "Seriously. I know you studied business in college. But you're like a magic cure. How do you do that?" she asked, then cursed herself for opening this can of worms. He probably learned how to give massages from a woman.

"Look, I could give you some line about how I've always been good with my hands, and it's true. But I'm pretty sure that the talent you just saw came from the fact that I put myself through college making pizzas."

She cracked up—of all the reasons to be good at massage, she'd never have picked *that* one. "Are you serious? You never told me that before."

"I was a pizza boy. I got a job at this local pizza joint near school, and I worked my ass off five nights a week making pies. Yep, I can knead dough like nobody's business."

"You are a hard worker. I'm impressed, too, that you put yourself through college."

"Paid every cent myself. I've just always believed you have to work for what you want in life."

"I believe that, too. My parents offered to help me with a down payment on my first house, but I wanted to do it myself. So as I was tending bar, then managing bars, I saved the money to get myself a little house. It's small, but it's mine, and I love it. And speaking of working hard," she said, shifting gears to a more serious note. "I have an idea for you."

"Okay, what is it?"

"Now I know you don't like to ask for help," she said, doing her best to be gentle but firm. "But I want to help you with your business."

He gave her a strange look as if she were speaking a foreign language. "What do you mean?"

"Well, you need to expand. You've hinted at that before. But you won't hire anyone because you got burned when that guy you worked with stole from one of your clients, right?"

"Right," he said, taking a step back, and she knew she was touching a nerve. Smith was very much man against the world, a true do-it-yourselfer.

"My sister runs my parents' winery and she just hired a bunch of new part-timers to help out. Day laborers. She said they're great and working out well. And I would really like to connect you with her and see if maybe you can hire some of them too."

"Yeah, but how do I know it'll all work out?" he asked, his voice wary.

"You don't, but she's good at her job and it seems to be going well so far."

His features softened. "I guess I can talk to her. I know Becker wants me to get moving on this. But you sure she only uses trustworthy guys?"

"Of course. Diane is very thorough about vetting them."

"All right. I'll talk to her and see if I can throw some work their way too," he said, then ran his hand gently along her arm. "Thank you for wanting to help. It means a lot to me."

He was starting to mean a lot to her, and that was scary. True feelings were more than she'd bargained for when she masterminded this week-long affair. That's why she had to stick to her guns, and be over and out after their one date. She'd miss him too much—their friendship and their fun—if they turned serious and then fell to pieces, as they surely would.

At the very least, though, she'd let herself fully enjoy their last night together. The week had neared its end, and she'd promised him one real date. They'd go out with a bang.

Chapter Ten

The restaurant overlooked the town square, tables spilling out onto the sidewalk, and tourists strolled by, weaving in and out of the shops, as they talked throughout the meal—he told her some of his favorite stories about absurd calls he'd gone on for the fire department, and she shared some of her silliest bar tales. She also let him know that she'd talked to Diane, who was eager to help him find some good hires, and wanted to chat on the phone with him tomorrow about next steps.

He was going to need to convince her that there would be a tomorrow for them.

As the waiter cleared their plates, Smith gestured to the square where some kids were playing Frisbee, couples sat on benches, and a statue of the Hidden Oaks founder presided over it all. "Soon, you'll be able to dunk me there."

"Damn straight. You know you're going down," she joked.

He leaned in closer to her, trailing his fingers down her

bare arm in the way he knew made her shiver. "Speaking of going down, I don't believe we've added that to our repertoire yet," he whispered in her ear. He knew he was supposed to be serious, but hell, he loved teasing her. He adored flirting with her. He could not resist being playful.

"Smith," she chided. "There are kids around."

"Well, I wasn't going to do it here. Unless you want me to."

"No. Not here. But aren't we going to a movie? You know, the whole real date thing."

"We had dinner. I can take you to a movie, or I can *take you*. And I can *have* you."

"You know you can have me that way. I'm just glad I have you all to myself for this week."

"You can have any part of me all to yourself."

She rolled her eyes. "Always innuendo with you."

"I can do innuendo or I can be in you." He turned serious then, because that's what she needed. "Jamie, I want you this week and every week. We've had a great date, haven't we?"

She bit her lip briefly, then nodded. "Yes," she said, as if she were admitting something difficult.

"I knew we would. We're good together, aren't we?"

"Smith," she said, as if his name was a warning.

"What? We have. It's just a fact of life. And the sooner you admit it, the better off we'll be. Go to the festival with me. On another date."

She laughed. "How about I just kiss you right now?" She placed her hands on his cheeks and captured his mouth with hers, like she was staking her claim to him. She gave him the kind of hard and hungry kiss that he liked to bestow on her, and it was as if the world had gone dark and she was all there was. He was swimming in her scent, in the fragrance of her neck, the sweet taste of her mouth, the fruity smell of shampoo in her hair. She was so pretty, so feminine, and so forward in the way she was owning their kiss in public. He shivered as her fingernails traced lines in his hair, as her tongue darted in and out of his mouth. She sucked on his bottom lip, lightly grazing her teeth into him. Then she stopped and nibbled on his ear, little flicks on his earlobe that made him growl. He slipped his hands underneath her shirt, pressing his palms against the small of her back. Her skin was so hot, and so was his, and he could no longer hold a single thought in his head that didn't have to do with getting her naked.

"Let's skip that movie," she said.

"If you insist on skipping the date part…"

"I do insist. I want you."

"Those are my three favorite words. Wait. So are these: *I live closer*," he said.

"Your house. Now."

Fifteen minutes later, they'd barely made it inside his home when she grabbed the waistband of his jeans and claimed his mouth again. Damn, she was a feisty one. He wanted to thank his lucky stars, because who would have thought that she'd be his perfect match in *and* out of the bedroom? He sure hoped she was seeing it too, from the way they chatted and had a good time, to *this*.

She pressed her lips against his in some kind of sweet devouring and trailed her hands down his shirt, yanking it loose from his jeans. She danced her fingertips across his stomach.

"I'm going to do my laundry on your abs." She mimed rubbing fabric across his midsection.

"You can use me any way you want," he teased, and even though he knew he needed to win her on all accounts, his body was in overdrive with desire right now. For her. "But I'm going to do something to you right now that I'm pretty sure you like a lot," he said, and kissed her back lightly, sliding the tip of his tongue across her lips in a way that made it clear what he planned to do next. "I love it when you ask for it. Will you ask for it?"

He pulled back to savor her reaction.

She breathed out hard. Closed her eyes. Opened them again. Swayed toward him. Her chest fell against his and he could feel her breasts through the fabric of her sweater. In a hungry voice, she rasped out, "Will you go down on me please?"

A grin slowly spread across his face. "I am at your service."

He spun her around so her back rested against the wall in his hallway.

• • •

If it were possible to die from desire, then this might be Jamie's last moment on earth. She wanted his touch so badly, it felt like a primal sort of need. An ache that had to be filled, and bless this man, he didn't make her wait. He slid a hand between her legs, pressing his palm against her damp panties.

Then two hands were under her skirt, and he stripped off her underwear in seconds. Before he kneeled down, he returned his hand to her wetness. She quivered, her whole body trembling at his touch. He brought her finger to his mouth and sucked on it. "Mmm," he said, shaking his head appreciatively. "You taste like you're dying for me to lick you all over and make you come on my tongue. Is that fair to say?"

Heat flared through her, threatening to turn her molten. She could barely speak, could only nod and breathe out a strangled "Yes."

He kneeled down, resting his strong hands on the insides of her thighs as he kissed her between her legs. His lips were made for this and he went down on her as if it was air, as if it was breath, as if the taste of her was the very thing he craved for sustenance and survival. He kissed and ran his tongue across her, and when she thought she couldn't bear any more ecstasy, he slid one strong finger inside her, and that was all it took.

She'd been hovering near the edge, teetering on the crest of a mind-blowing orgasm, and with one more touch, and one more delicious slide across her, she was there, the pressure of her climax both exquisitely intense and freeing, as she called his name over and over. She grabbed his hair, pulling his face against her, as she came on his tongue.

She flashed back to their other times. He'd been rough and hard, and she'd loved that. But just now, she'd seen another side of his touch. He savored her, he delighted in her, he cherished her. She loved all these sides of him.

Soon, he rose, and though he looked pleased with his work, he also looked at her tenderly, and with such passion, she knew there was no turning back. Not from hope, and not from the possibility of heartbreak. She'd tried to keep him at arm's length, but that had been all for naught. She craved him in every way, and while she knew this was ending, she wanted this time with him to be more than just sex.

Later, when they fell asleep together in his bed, she

drifted off, thinking how very much she liked being in his arms.

That was the problem. It was absolutely the biggest problem she faced right now. She'd painted herself into a corner, and she had no idea how to get out.

Chapter Eleven

As she walked into The Panting Dog the next day, her heart fluttered at the prospect of seeing him there, and she wanted to tell the dumb organ to settle down. She had no clue what to do or say around him anymore. She didn't know what they were, or whether they were coming or going. She was rudderless when it came to him, and that scared the heck out of her.

Focus on the friendship, she reminded herself. That was the most important part.

She found him quickly in the back of the bar, tools in hands.

"How did everything go with Diane?" she asked as she walked up to him, with her best friendly face on.

"Great. I think she's going to be a tremendous help."

"Good. I'm happy to hear that. I'm seeing her later for dinner at my parents' house, so I'm sure she can give me more details."

"Hey Jamie. I've got an idea," he said, and she detected a touch of nerves in his tone, but he continued stroking her arm, as if that action steadied him.

"What's your idea?"

"Why don't you bring me along to dinner? I would really love it if you'd invite me to spend time with you and your parents and your sister," he said.

Jamie froze. Like a computer with the blue screen of death. Her lips parted and she tried to speak but no words came. Then she knew. With blazing certainty. This was the line she didn't want to cross. Because if she did, she'd be all in, and that was as good as asking for her heart to be broken. It was one thing to talk to Diane about his work needs, but entirely another to invite Smith into her world. Inviting him in meant they were real, and being real meant she'd get hurt. Sure, he knew Diane—Hidden Oaks was a small town—but they didn't hang out together. If she brought him into her family as a romantic interest then she was admitting out loud that he was just that—more than a late-night affair. If he was more than an affair, he'd leave her in the dust soon enough.

Leave her with nothing to show for it.

She needed to move him back to the friend zone. Officially. It was better this way. Safer this way. At least they'd have something if they stayed friends.

Her chest felt heavy as she shook her head. "I don't think that's such a good idea. Let's just keep this thing between you and me for now. Friends and all," she added, as if to justify her reasons. She had to focus on the friendship simply to preserve it.

Something dark passed over his eyes, but then he nodded

quickly, fixing a serious look on his face. He let go of her arm.

• • •

Smith prided himself on being easygoing. He tried hard not to let things get to him. And he certainly wasn't known for a short temper. So it took every ounce of self-control not to say something hurtful to match what he felt inside.

Through gritted teeth, he spoke under his breath. "So let me see if I understand this. I'm good enough for you to get down on your knees in my hallway. To help with business. And you'll even happily play Mad Libs in my truck," he said, watching as she cringed with his reminders of all they'd done. "But having dinner with your sister is where you draw the line?"

"Smith," she said, fidgeting with the cuffs of her sweater, as she tried desperately to look anywhere but in his eyes.

"Smith what?" he asked sharply.

"It's not like that."

"Then what is it like? Enlighten me."

"We're not doing a relationship," she said, her voice cool and even. "So I don't know why we'd do that. We're friends, and I want to stay that way."

"You told me you think I'm just fun and easygoing, but you also said you wanted serious. I'm trying to be serious by spending time with you and your family. To show you I can be that guy. I thought that's what you wanted."

"I do," she said in a careful voice, as if it were a question.

The silence clung to him, and in the span of several painful seconds, the answer to her question dawned on him.

"Just not with me," he said, and he didn't bother to keep

the anger from his voice this time. He hadn't planned for this, but after last night, and the way they connected today, he didn't expect this kind of brush-off.

"That's not it."

"Were you just slumming it with me in the bedroom?"

She furrowed her brows. "What?"

Anger and shame rolled through him, fueling his words. "You liked fucking me because I'm not proper; I'm not a poet; I'm not the romantic, sensitive, perfect guy. You like the wild side. But I'm never gonna be the kind of guy you want to take home to your parents."

Her lips parted, and she tried to say something but nothing came out. Her mouth hung open as if she were struggling to find an answer. And that was all the answer he needed. It had been a week, and he thought he'd won both her heart and her body, but when it came right down to it, he was only the dirty-talking fireman to her. He was a joyride, a wild and dirty escape for her. He knew he shouldn't be surprised—she'd laid down the rules, after all: one week of sex, and that week had drawn to a close.

He stripped the anger from his voice. He didn't want her to know how much he cared. So much that her dismissal of him felt like a hard punch in the ribs. "I get it. It's cool. And, I really appreciate the offer of help from your sister. But I have this under control. And, by the way, it's been a fun week, hasn't it? But it's over now, so thanks for the memories, and I need to get back to work so I can finish this bar and get out of your way."

"That's not what I meant," she said, her lips quivering, her eyes brimming.

He turned around, jammed the headphones back on his

ears, and drowned out thoughts of her as he listened to music and forced himself to do nothing but work, work, work all day so he could be done with this project and have one less chance of running into Jamie.

Chapter Twelve

More games. More music. Maybe a live band.

That was as much as Jamie picked up during the impromptu meeting. Because her mind was elsewhere.

"What do you think, Jamie? You know this town well. Which of those ideas would work best?"

The question came from Becker, as he picked up his glass of beer and took a drink. It was the end of the night, The Panting Dog was closed, and Becker, Kaitlyn, and Jamie were discussing final ideas for the Spring Festival.

Correction: Supposed to be.

Jamie kept replaying the afternoon run-in with Smith, trying to figure out where she'd gone wrong. Smith was so laid-back and cool, so devil-may-care, that it had surprised her to learn he did care. A lot.

"A band would be great," she said, seizing onto the last suggestion. She wanted to play a vital role in the operations of The Panting Dog. She couldn't let on that she'd been drifting off during this whole conversation, thinking of Smith the entire time. The way he made her laugh. The way he teased her. How he understood her, and what made her tick, in ways no one else did. How he liked all sides of her, and how he had such a sweet, tender side too.

Had she been wrong about him and quick to judge? Was it possible that she could have a relationship with him? That he could commit the way she wanted?

She feared the answer was yes.

She'd been falling for him hard, but when he asked to spend time with her family, she balked. Not because she was embarrassed of him, but because she didn't know how to admit that she'd gone all in. That there were no strings *unattached* anymore.

• • •

As she unlocked her door an hour later, she found herself wondering what Smith was doing without her. The last several nights they'd been together. Now they weren't, and her house felt dreadfully alone.

She tried her usual techniques to busy her mind before bed. She picked up her favorite books. She thumbed through Browning, Donne, and Shakespeare. She cued up Ron Burgundy. She even picked up the phone to call her sister, but she realized it was past eleven and too late to ring Diane. She scrolled listlessly through her phone, then noticed a text from Megan. "*It's over with Jason. I'm coming back to town.*"

Jamie sat up ramrod straight and called her friend instantly.

"What's going on?"

Megan told her everything—how she'd tried hard to make things work but Jason had been more in love with substances than with her.

"I'm so sorry, sweetie. That sucks. But can I tell you how happy I am to be able to see you again soon? Is that terribly selfish of me?"

Megan laughed. "No, it's not selfish, because I can't wait to see you, either."

"You need to stop by the second you get to town. Plus, I want you to come see The Panting Dog. It wasn't around when you were here and my boss is super hot."

"You're already trying to set me up," Megan said. "Besides, if he's so hot, why aren't you after him?"

"Well, that's the thing," she said, taking a deep breath and deciding to lay it all out. She wasn't embarrassed this time. She wasn't hiding Smith anymore. She needed to talk about him because he mattered to her. "There's someone else."

She told Megan the whole story from start to finish. "What do you think?"

"I leave town and exciting things happen, that's what I think."

"So what do I do? I miss him," she said, feeling his absence like an empty ache inside her.

"And you're ready for a relationship with him?"

Her heart beat faster at the thought, crazy as it was. She'd be a fool to give up this chance at something more. She knew that now. "Yeah, I think I am."

"Then there's only one thing to do. Apologize. Lay it on the line for him."

"How?"

"Think of a way that matters to him."

Jamie mulled over those words, and within minutes she knew the perfect way to say she was sorry to the man who'd unexpectedly stolen her heart.

• • •

Nerves fluttered recklessly in her belly as she walked up the steps to Smith's home. His truck was in the driveway, and she hoped so hard that he'd answer. She knocked and waited and waited and waited, the seconds stretching interminably as she shifted back and forth in her boots, hoping he would accept her apology.

When he opened the door, his face was inscrutable. He looked tired, but that wasn't surprising. He'd been working late the night before to finish the bar. But he looked beautiful, too. As gorgeous as the times she'd lusted for him, and even more so now that her feelings had transformed from lust to something far deeper.

"Hi," she said, the word coming out all jumpy sounding. But she soldiered on, unfolding the piece of paper in her hand. "I wrote you a Mad Lib. I call it Mad Lib poetry and I hope you'll bear with me as I read it."

The corners of his lips quirked up in curiosity and she began.

"I'm sorry—Name of Person—*Sexiest and Sweetest and Funniest Man I've Ever Known*. About the—Adjective—*idiotic* thing I did yesterday. I hope you'll accept my—Adjective—*heartfelt* apology as well as some—Plural Noun—*monkeys*," she read, and glanced up to see his eyes sparkling with recognition.

"Monkeys gets 'em every time," he whispered, then tipped his forehead to the paper so she kept going.

"This is my way of saying I'm a—Self-Deprecating-Title—*Dunce*. And if you'll still have me, I'd like to go on another—Adjective—*wonderful, romantic, fun, fantastic* date with you. And my big sister will join us for drinks because I'm not embarrassed of you. I was—insert words to describe how you felt when you were being a dunce—*scared of getting hurt*. And I really hope you'll accept this attempt at saying let's try with strings all attached," she said, eagerly awaiting his answer.

"Darlin', I have always been all in, and I could not be happier to give this a go for real," he said, then pulled her in for a deep and devouring kiss that blotted out the whole wide world and turned her knees weak. Exactly as a kiss should do. "And incidentally, that was four adjectives rather than one for our second date tomorrow."

"Then let's make it four times as good," she said.

"We will."

Chapter Thirteen

Their first real date was better than the last one, and that had been a damn good one. This time, they'd gone bowling, drank beers, and laughed the whole time. He beat her in one game, and she beat him in the next, and then he'd finished off the final round with several strikes. She didn't mind losing to him, because she knew she was winning being with him, and she was glad they were all in.

Now, they were at her house. She shut and locked her front door, took his hand, and led him back to her bedroom for the first time.

She turned on the light and watched him as he took in her room. The dark red comforter on her king-size bed, because she liked to sleep splayed out like a starfish, the well-worn books on her nightstand. Then the framed pictures of her and her parents, her sister, and Tennyson. Finally, there was the note card he'd given her, lying on her nightstand.

Another time.

"You kept it," he remarked, with wonder in his voice.

"I did. Because it was from you. 'The promise of another time, and that time is now.'" She reached for the bottom of his shirt and tugged it off. She'd seen him shirtless plenty of times, but now, here, in her bedroom, the sight of his naked torso—so muscular and cut—was a heady one.

He kicked off his shoes. She unzipped his jeans and let them fall to the floor. She'd seen him naked before but she didn't think she'd tire of the sight. Every inch of him, every ounce, was the embodiment of masculine perfection. Strong arms, broad chest, abs she wanted to lick, fabulous legs, and then the pièce de résistance—that perfect cock, long, thick, and hard as a rock for her.

But he was more than just a beautiful body now. More than merely the man she'd lusted after for months, and then slept with on a whim one heady night in a bar. He was the man she'd let into her life, her family, her home. And though they'd had sex several times already, this time felt different.

"I kind of feel like this is our first time," she said, whispering it like an admission.

"I feel the same," he said, as he gently stripped off her sweater and unhooked her bra. She shimmied out of her skirt. He stepped back to look at her, taking her in, his eyes roaming every inch of her, and the look in them was heated and full of something more too. The *more* that she'd once tried to deny. But now wanted to embrace.

He'd spent so much time telling her nice things, sweet things, pretty things, and now she wanted to return his affection. To let him know this had never been a one-way street. She trailed her fingertips down his chest, watching as he hitched in a breath. "You're beautiful to me," she said.

"All of you."

His chest rose and fell, and his lips curved up. He closed his eyes briefly as she traced a line from his hip to his butt. "I love the way you touch me," he said in a hot, hoarse voice, and though she loved his dirty mouth, she loved this part too—the one that was patently honest. "And I need you now."

She held up her index finger, raced into the bathroom, found a condom packet under the sink, and returned with it.

She pushed him gently onto the bed, then ran her hand over him, and his cock twitched against her as she rolled on the condom. She straddled him and he placed his hands on her hips as she lowered onto him, his eyes closing in pleasure.

. . .

She felt amazing. So wet, so warm, so tight as she surrounded him. She tensed briefly as she took him all the way in, then exhaled and sank farther down. He held her hips, moving her slowly on him. He wanted to savor the feeling of being inside her like this. The first time after admitting they were something more. He kept his gaze on her as she rode him, her long hair falling against her back, making her look even sexier, if that were possible. He hadn't thought it was, but now he knew he'd been wrong. She was the most beautiful woman he'd ever seen, and she was his. The look in her eyes was one of desire, but he saw her vulnerability, too, the way she'd stripped bare her fears, finally letting him in. And he felt even more for her because of that. Because she trusted him, and he was never going to hurt her.

He was only ever going to make her feel good.

He held onto her hips, matching her rhythm, but he needed her body against his completely. "I want to feel you against me as you ride me."

She leaned closer, her breasts brushing against his chest now, her mouth near his. She moved her hips slowly, up and down, like a tease. Making him groan, making him roll his eyes back in his head.

"Do you like it when I take you slow like this?" she asked, rising up on him, then taking him all the way inside her, and grinding her hips on him.

"I like that you're a talker. That you give it right back to me."

"I love giving it back to you," she said, drawing up her hips, again, then slamming down on him. "Or would you rather I fuck you hard?" she said, swearing for the first time with him. She gasped at her own use of a dirty word and his eyes widened.

"Oh, you know that's only going to get me going even more," he said.

She pinned his wrists over his head while pumping her hips against him. "Good. I like getting you going. I like being the only one who can make you feel this way."

"You are. The only one. Hold me down and press your beautiful body against mine," he said as she rode him, picking up the pace, building into a frenzy, taking him right there with her, his body becoming an inferno as he watched her move on him. He could barely stand it. He grabbed her ass, then held onto her as he switched positions, staying inside her the whole time as he moved her underneath him.

"Wrap your legs tight around me, and I'm going hold your hands down until you come," he said, needing to take charge again.

She raised her arms above her head, eagerly inviting him to take over. He held her wrists in one hand as she arched her back.

"Do you want me to make you come soon?"

"I do," she said in between pants.

"Tell me how much you want me to drive you wild right now."

"Oh god, Smith. I want you so much," she said, those eyes dark as she became a wild woman in bed. "Take me so hard I'll still feel you tomorrow."

His senses went into overdrive. His body was alive with fire and heat. Every nerve, every muscle, every brain cell was focused on one thing—pleasing her.

"I want you to say my name when you're coming on me, got that?" he said, as he filled her to the hilt, her breath catching as she gasped. She was getting closer, and he was going to bring her over the edge any second.

"You're so sexy, it's killing me," she said, moaning. "You make me feel so good."

She spread her legs even wider, wrapping them around his ass.

"You know why I make you feel this way?"

"Because I'm crazy for you," she said, answering him with words he'd always wanted to hear.

"God, that makes me so happy."

She held on tight, drawing him as far into her as she could take him, and then looked him in the eyes, her mouth forming a perfect O as she cried out.

"Smith."

That was it. Just his name. That was all she could manage,

and he watched her as she shuddered. Then again, even louder, as he drove into her, his own orgasm coursing through him, following hers. Then he collapsed onto her, burying his face in her hair.

· · ·

Once was never enough. So they went for seconds, and then thirds sometime in the middle of the night. When morning rolled around, he hopped into her shower, and she joined him, surprising him by kneeling down and taking him in her mouth.

"Best. Shower. Ever," he declared when she finished, and turned off the water.

As he toweled off, he stopped to check his phone. He scrolled through his messages casually, then seemed to stop and study one. His shoulders tightened. "I have to get going. I'm late. I have another construction job I'm working on over on Meadow Lane."

She furrowed her brow. "But I thought you were hiring some guys to help. So you don't have to do everything yourself."

"I am," he said, tapping her nose playfully. "But they're not hired yet, so it's still on my shoulders. And then it's my afternoon at the Burn Center so I am a busy boy."

"I love that you do that," she said, as she pulled on a long T-shirt, then sat cross-legged on her bed, watching him dress.

"So when will I see you again?" he asked as he zipped up his jeans.

"I'm working this afternoon too. Day shift. What about

tomorrow?"

"What about tonight?"

She couldn't suppress a grin. Nothing would be better than seeing him again so soon now that they were together for real.

"Well, it's the first night of the festival. Don't you need to be dunked?"

"Tomorrow night is for dunking. Tonight I am taking my woman to the Spring Festival."

His woman. She never thought she'd let herself go there. But here she was, and the words—the title—made her feel as if a fleet of hummingbirds had taken flight in her body.

She'd fallen for him. Against her better judgment. Against all her plans to do the opposite. He'd put himself out there many times for her. She wanted to do the same, and wanted it to be more than her apology the other night, more than asking him on a date. She met his gaze, those blazing blue eyes like a clear sky. A spark raced inside her, and this time it was from her heart, not just her body. She looked at him, scared but hopeful because she was going to open her heart no matter what. He'd earned it many times over.

She walked him to the door, her insides knotted as she practiced the words in her head first. He was about to step outside, but she grabbed his arm. "I'm falling for you," she said, feeling as if she'd just exposed her hiding place to the enemy.

His phone lit up with a message. He glanced at it in his hand, then at her. He pecked her on the forehead then rushed down the steps. "I need to go, darlin'."

He took off, leaving her on the porch, feeling thoroughly perplexed.

Chapter Fourteen

Everything is fine. He's not with another woman. He's just busy. You didn't scare him off.

All morning she was filled with worry. But she repeated her mantra, trying to talk herself down. By the time she left for work an hour later, she almost believed it.

The jitters were simply new lover nerves. The fact that he hadn't returned her *I'm falling for you* wasn't something to worry about. They were going to the Spring Festival together tonight; they'd play Skee-Ball, have some cotton candy, and then sneak off to an alley somewhere for a quickie.

Jamie smiled to herself, liking that image. Glad, too, that she'd talked herself down from pointless fears.

On the walk to work, her phone buzzed, and she removed it from her purse to check the message.

Her shoulders fell as she read it.

Hey baby. Can we reschedule? Something came up

that I have to take care of NOW. Call you later.

She looked at the time. It was ten thirty in the morning. What could possibly have come up that he had to take care of now? A fire? God forbid. But if it was a fire, she'd have heard sirens, and he'd have said so.

Jamie jammed the phone back into her bag. It had to be an error. A missent message. He couldn't possibly be canceling their date.

Or could he?

She walked through town, looking in familiar store windows on her way to The Panting Dog, trying to reassure herself that she could trust him. He was reliable. He was serious. But already her heart was racing at a rabbit's pace because this was her fear. That once she went all in, he'd pull out. He'd love her and leave her like he did with the other ladies. As she stopped at a red light, she noticed a familiar profile at the end of the next block. A pretty brunette. An even more beautiful blond man. Then he opened Cara's car door for her, walked around to the passenger side, and drove off with her.

This is what came up? He needed to spend time with Cara when he claimed he was working and volunteering?

She blinked and squeezed her eyes shut, then open, as if that would hold back the stupid tears.

• • •

"Whoa. Easy there."

Jamie lifted her eyes to Becker as she slammed a glass down hard on the bar. She'd just cleaned the glass, and was now prepping for the dinner shift at The Panting Dog.

"Sorry," she said, lowering her gaze. She didn't want her boss to know she was pissed and hurt, though she was having the hardest time keeping her emotions hidden.

"Whatever it is, let's just dial it down a notch," he said in a gentle voice.

But she had to stay mad. Anger was a shield, and if she let it fall, she'd break down, and she'd deserve it. She was an idiot for letting him in. He had no interest in a real relationship at all. Hell, he had no real interest in *her* seeing as how he had a perfect chance to tell her he was falling too and he didn't. This must be his M.O. and now she was on the receiving end of love 'em and leave 'em. Screw their friendship. To hell if they were going to be able to stay friends now.

But Becker was a good guy and her boss, so she couldn't take it out on him. She stared at a bottle on the counter, wanting to throw it across the room, watch it explode and take the hurt with it.

"You okay?" he asked.

She was not okay. She was not okay in any way, shape, or form. "Yeah, totally," she lied and scrambled for something else to talk about. "My friend is moving back here soon. I can't wait to see her," she said, trying to focus on anything but Smith and the fact that she hadn't heard a word all day. She was wound up now, her insides a twisted mess of worry and regret. She'd been played like a fool, hadn't she? Believing she was special, and being left when it suited him.

She didn't know what she'd do when she saw him again, but she'd have to figure it out now because he strolled in the door, looking quite pleased with himself. He held his arms out wide, as if he were leading a victory parade.

"Good evening, ladies and gentlemen," he said, nodding to Becker. "But especially to the lovely lady behind the bar."

Jamie took the deepest breath she'd ever taken in her life, letting the hurt that came with it expand throughout her entire body. She picked up the bottle of wine that had gone unopened, whirled around, and marched to the back room to tuck it away. Seconds later, she felt a hand on her shoulder. She shrugged it off.

"Hey, darlin', you okay?"

"Don't 'hey, darlin'' me."

He didn't seem to process what she'd just said, because he reached for her, trying to touch her hair, but she slipped away from his grasp.

"I texted to tell you I was on my way back."

"On your way back? From where? From your construction job? From the Burn Center? Or just from getting away from me as soon as you possibly could?"

"Excuse me?"

"You took off like you couldn't wait to leave this morning. You knew this was hard for me, taking a chance like this, and we're supposed to be friends. You're supposed to be able to be honest with me, but instead you just left, and—" she said, and like a strong wind that came out of nowhere, all her anger was gone, and in its place were thick, hot tears rolling down her cheeks. "Was it all just about sex after all?"

"Jamie, no, I swear. It's more than that. You have to believe me. You have to trust me," he said, reaching out to grab her arm.

But she couldn't even trust herself or her own emotions. Because she'd never expected to feel so much for him, and now she felt like a fool.

"I have to go," she said and she stalked off, grabbing her bag from behind the counter, uttering a quick good-bye to Becker and telling Kaitlyn she needed to go since her shift was over. She rushed outside, greeted by the laughter and music and noise from the Spring Festival across the street, already underway in the town square.

She wished it were night, and a dark sky would shadow the tears that slid down her cheeks.

• • •

"Man, I will never understand women," Smith said, pulling up a stool and parking himself on it.

Becker chuckled and filled a glass from the tap, sliding it over. "Buddy, I don't know any man who truly does, so join the club."

"I don't get them. Not one bit," he said, taking a long swallow of the cold beer. Damn, that tasted good. He tapped the side of the glass. "This? Beer? I understand beer. And I understand fires and how to fight them. And I understand hammering nails into wood. But women?" He shook his head several times.

"Wish I could help you. I'm happy to try, though, if you want to lay it on me," Becker said, resting his hands on the bar counter. "After all, I'm kind of playing bartender here tonight."

Smith hadn't told his friend any details yet, and Jamie was his employee, so he erred on the side of caution, not using names. "There's this woman," he began.

"Yeah, I'm clear on that part," Becker said with a wry

laugh.

"And she wasn't sure about going out with me, thought I wasn't the relationship type. That I couldn't be serious. But we started to get close, and now she's worried I don't really care about her in the same way."

Becker raised an eyebrow. "But you do, right?"

"Yes. Fuck yes. But she didn't even give me a chance to explain. And that's what makes me crazy. She took off the first time we were together, and now she did it again. She never gives me a damn chance."

Becker started wiping down the counter. "Listen. It's a new relationship. You just need to be honest with her. Tell her how you feel, and reassure her—"

"But she walked out when I tried to tell her," he said, crossing his arms over his chest. "And that makes me wonder if it's worth it. Or if she's just going to flip every time something happens."

"Was she crying?"

He flashed back to her exodus, recalling the way her eyes started to fill with tears. "Yeah," he said tentatively, not sure what Becker was getting at.

"Then let me tell you something. She likes you and she's scared. And if you like her too, then you need to go make things right," Becker said, looking him square in the eyes, man to man. "Do you want to make things right?"

That was the question. Did he? He was pretty sure he did earlier in the day, given what he'd been up to. He wanted Jamie to trust him, though, to have faith that he was a good guy who'd treat her right. Completely. As he analyzed the situation, he reminded himself that last night was their first real date. Everything was still new between them. They were learning how to be together. She was worried and nervous, and his buddy was right. He needed to reassure her. If he did it now, and proved himself now, they could keep moving forward on solid footing. He'd tried hard to win her heart in the last week, pushing past his own fears about how she felt, what their relationship would do to their friendship, and even about growing his own business. If Jamie made the effort to do a Mad Libs apology and set up a dinner with her sister as a show of faith, then he damn well needed to let her know that she could keep trusting him.

"Oh, and I know you're talking about Jamie," Becker said with a knowing glint in his eye. "I see the way she looks at you. She's a good one, Smith. Go make things right."

He set down his glass on the counter and extended a hand. "Thank you for kicking me in the ass."

"Anytime."

• • •

"Can I have another, please?"

The small voice rose up to Jamie's ears.

"Of course you can," she answered, doing her best to be as chipper as could be. Her arms were covered in a fine mist of pink sugar. Jamie reached for a paper tube, dipped it into the sugar-filled tin, and began swirling. But her cotton candy creations were a mess tonight. Lumpy and thin and not the pillowy clouds she was known for.

She swept the tube through the spinning sugar, trying to make an ideal treat for the child, but her hurt was stronger. She pushed hard against the side of the machine, and the paper tube shot out of her hand, landing on the grass.

"Oh crap," she said, bending down to grab it.

"Hey, let me finish," her sister said gently. Diane started over, recreating the treat and handing it to the child.

The Spring Festival was in full swing, and a pop band played upbeat tunes in the gazebo, as families, children, and couples played games and danced to the music. When the line ebbed at the cotton candy stand, Diane turned to her. "What's going on? You're not yourself tonight."

"Oh, it's nothing. Just a rough day at work," she said, glancing away so her sister couldn't read the lie.

Diane reached for her shoulder. Squeezed it. "Hey. Talk to me. I'm your big sister. I know you didn't have a rough day at work. You never have rough days at work. You love your job. You love your life. Is this about Smith?"

Jamie sighed heavily, as if all the tension inside her was spilling out too. Along with the stupid tears she never wanted to shed for him. "You were right when you said to be careful. I should have listened," she said, hanging her head low.

"What do you mean?"

"I trusted him. I let him in. And you warned me way back when. But then I told him this morning that I was falling for him, and he said *nothing* in response. Actually, he said, 'I have to go,' and that's worse than nothing," she said, fighting back more tears as the band from the gazebo launched into a pop song about second chances. She clenched her jaw, wishing they were playing breakup tunes because that's what she needed now. "I should have known better."

Diane smoothed out her hair and brought her in for a hug. "Smith is a good guy. I've been talking to him a lot lately because of the hires he's making."

"Then why did he just leave? Was it only about the sex

after all? And he's not serious about me?"

"Maybe he had a reason," Diane said evasively, but with a twinkle in her eyes.

Jamie narrowed her eyes and stared at her sister, trying to see inside and make sense of the nonsense coming out of Diane's mouth. "Hello? Where is my sister who told me to be careful?"

"I did tell you to be careful, and I stand by that. I also stand by what I said about him being crazy for you. Give him a chance. I think the man knows you pretty well."

Before she could respond, she heard something scampering toward her, and when she looked down she saw the most adorable furry face she'd ever seen. A German shepherd puppy with a dark snout, pointy ears, and huge, fluffy paws. His mouth lolled open and his tongue hung out, giving him the perfect puppy smile. He looked vaguely familiar, like the dog on the waiting list.

"Have you ever seen a more adorable creature?" she said to Diane, a surge of happiness returning to her, thanks to the little canine.

"He's pretty damn cute."

The dog licked Jamie's leg and she laughed at the feel of the rough tongue on her skin. "I probably have cotton candy on my leg too," she said, then noticed the little puppy had a note attached to his collar. With her name on it. In familiar handwriting. Her heart thumped hard, and all the happiness that had escaped her earlier came crashing back into her like a comet. She reached for the note with shaky, hopeful fingers.

Her heart dared to skip a beat. She trembled and opened it.

I'm falling for you too.

She looked up to see Smith holding a leather leash and wearing a massive grin.

"I believe this is the dog you wanted, ma'am?"

She clapped her hand over her mouth. She glanced from the dog to Smith to the note. Then she felt Diane's hand on her shoulder. "Told you so."

Jamie stood. "Did you know about this?"

Diane nodded. "We texted this morning."

"You knew all along?" Her mouth hung open.

"I did," she said with a huge grin.

Jamie looked at Smith, and she couldn't stop smiling either. "That's why you were so into your phone this morning?"

"I wanted to make sure she thought it was a good idea to get you the dog you wanted. And she said yes. So I had the big sister approval before I got him for you."

"But how did you get him?"

The puppy rubbed his snout against Jamie's leg and started licking again. She laughed and picked him up.

"I'll tell you how. But we need to set some ground rules first."

• • •

Smith had the canine trump card, and he was pretty damn sure Jamie was bending his way again. But he was going to need to let her know once and for all how he felt about her.

"Now, listen. I texted you. I told you something came up. And I meant it. *This* came up."

The puppy barked. A loud sound for such a young dog.

"I think he wants you to hold him," he said, and she

scooped him up and hugged him tight. "I didn't tell you where I was because I was with Cara picking up this gift for you. She happens to know all the shelters in Northern California, and she made some calls, and made sure you got the dog you were on the waiting list for. And that's why I was so damn preoccupied with my phone this morning, texting her, and texting your sister."

"You did all that for me?" she said, with something like wonder in her voice.

"Don't you get it? I'm crazy for you. And I should have told you this morning when you told me how you felt, but all I wanted to do was get you this dog. To show you how well I know you and how committed I can be to you."

"I was just so scared. I'd let you in and I want you in, but I thought you only wanted the no-strings part and that once you got the strings, you wanted to cut them off."

He laughed. "I want all those strings wrapped around me. Maybe with a leash, too. Now give this little guy some attention," he said, nodding to the dog.

She stroked the puppy between his small pointy ears, then kissed him once on the head. "I love him already," she said. Then she spoke quietly, looking contrite. "Will you forgive me for walking off again?"

"I hauled ass to San Jose when I heard we could get him. And I frigging hate San Jose. It was a six-hour drive round trip with all the traffic," he said. "I should have taken a moment on your front step and told you I was falling for you too, but I was so damn excited to get you the thing you've wanted most. For you, Jamie. I wanted you to have this dog for no other reason than I am damn crazy about you and only you, and nothing is going to change that."

A grin played on her lips. "This dog *is* the thing I've wanted most. But there's something else I want, too. Someone else."

"You'd better want me," he said, as if giving her a command. Then he softened. "So what are we going to name him?"

We.

They were a we.

Jamie studied the puppy in her arms. "How about Chance? Because you always told me to give you a chance."

He nodded, liking the name. "I think that's a most excellent name for a most excellent dog. Now, come dance with me," he said, tipping his forehead toward the gazebo as the band started on a slow song.

"But I have to make the cotton candy," she said.

Diane tapped her shoulder. "I can handle the cotton candy. Go dance with your man and your dog."

• • •

As they swayed under the stars, the dog played at their feet.

"And to think, it all started when you asked me to dance at the kickoff party," she said, tucking her face in the crook of his neck.

"And then we did many other things."

"Speaking of," she said. "Maybe we can get out of here soon."

"That's my woman. Coming back for more."

"So much more," she said. She grinned at him, then the dog, at their feet. "Smith, I'm glad I took a chance on you."

Acknowledgments

Thank you to all my readers who I adore to the ends of the earth and back! A big thanks to the editors at Entangled and to my agent Michelle for making this opportunity possible. Endless affection and hugs to my loving family, to the world's two most amazing dogs, and most of all to Lexi, Kendall, Sawyer, Monica, Violet, Melody, and Jessie for the NWB. I love you ladies like crazy!

About the Author

Lauren Blakely writes sexy contemporary romance novels with heat, heart, and humor, and many of her books have appeared on the *New York Times*, USA TODAY, Amazon, Barnes and Noble, and iBooks bestseller lists. Like the heroine in her novel, *Far Too Tempting*, she thinks life should be filled with family, laughter, and the kind of love that love songs promise. Lauren lives in California with her husband, children, and dogs. She loves hearing from readers! Her novels include *Caught Up In Us, Pretending He's Mine, Playing With Her Heart, Trophy Husband, Far Too Tempting, The Thrill of It, Every Second With You, Night After Night,* and *After This Night*. She also writes for young adults under the name Daisy Whitney.